LOVE OF A LIFETIME

Love of a Lifetime

AN ABUNDANCE SERIES PREQUEL

SALLY BAYLESS

KIMBERLIN BELLE PUBLISHING

Printed in the United States of America
ISBN: 978-1-946034-16-8

Originally published as *Love, Lies, and Homemade Pie,* © 2019 by Sally Bayless.

Kimberlin Belle Publishing
Contact: admin@kimberlinbelle.com

Scripture quotations are taken from The Living Bible copyright © 1971. Used by permission of Tyndale House Publishers, Inc., Carol Stream, Illinois 60188. All rights reserved.

Publisher's Note: This is a work of fiction. Names, characters, places, and incidents are a product of the author's imagination. Locales and public names are sometimes used for atmospheric purposes. Any resemblance to actual people, living or dead, or to businesses, companies, events, institutions, or locales is completely coincidental.

Cover Design © Jennifer Zemanek/Seedlings Design Studio

and may you be able to feel and understand, as all God's children should, how long, how wide, how deep, and how high his love really is;

Ephesians 3:18

Chapter One

Fear can really do a person in.

Oh, a little caution—the kind that makes a driver keep both eyes on the road—is a good thing.

But too much fear can ruin a person's life.

And starting today, at age twenty-seven, Cara Smith was building a new life, trying to put fear behind her and become the person she wanted to be.

Driving along the rural Missouri highway, she passed a sign for Abundance—the town where she'd chosen to begin that new life—and she attempted to push the pesky tickle of fear away. Then she took another look, noticing a green Lincoln Continental sprawled on the edge of the road.

A woman in a red business suit stood by the raised hood of the vehicle, waving her arms.

The smart thing to do, the cautious thing to do, since Cara was traveling alone, was to stop at the next gas station and ask the attendant to call the highway patrol.

But something about the woman radiated small-town propriety. Slightly frazzled small-town propriety, but propriety nonetheless. And she had two little kids in her backseat.

Cara eased her foot onto the brake. Being smart and cautious was one thing. Being downright unhelpful was another. Besides, wasn't her new life all about being brave? She pulled her white Volare onto the shoulder and turned off the engine.

The woman from the Lincoln hurried to Cara's passenger-side door. She looked about sixty, and her face shone with perspiration. Her hair, which probably began the day with a thick layer of Final Net, drooped on one side. Clearly, she'd chosen that red suit with its formidable shoulder pads because she'd believed she'd spend this sticky August day in air conditioning, not on the side of the road.

Cara reached across the passenger seat and cranked down the window.

"Thanks for stopping," the woman said. "Could you send someone to help? Or give my granddaughters and me a ride into town?" She gestured to the back seat of her car, where two girls who appeared to be identical twins peered out.

"What do you think is wrong?"

"I have no idea. It just died." She glared at the Lincoln, then looked back at Cara. "I'm Imogene Findley, by the way, the mayor of Abundance, that little town up ahead."

"Pleased to meet you. I'm An—uh—Cara Smith." Cara gave a quick smile, hopefully covering her slip, then glanced once more toward the Lincoln. "I'll gladly give you a lift, but I'd like to look at your car first. I'm pretty good with engines."

"If you think you can fix it, please, go ahead," Imogene said, but skepticism flickered across her eyes.

For a female mayor, Imogene didn't seem very confident in the abilities of a woman. And she should be. It was 1980 after all.

Granted, Cara wasn't a professional mechanic. But when a girl was raised by a father on his own, a somewhat distant father at that, then a shared understanding of engines became a way to connect. And, as she'd learned when she grew older, a knowledge of machinery was a handy thing to have.

Behind Imogene, one of the little girls waved from the back seat, her brown pigtails bouncing.

Cara waved back, waited until a pickup truck passed, and climbed out of her Volare. "If I can't take care of it in ten minutes, I'll drive you into town."

"Thanks. That would be great." Imogene gestured to her car. "I'm going to get back in to keep an eye on the girls."

Cara nodded, dug through the emergency supplies in her trunk for a rag, then went to the front of the Lincoln and studied the engine. A lock of hair—red hair—that had escaped her ponytail fell forward, and she pushed it behind her ear. A new hair color, a new name... The changes still tripped her up. If she was going to keep her identity a secret, she needed to get used to her new self. Fast.

For now, she should focus on this engine. Was it the radiator? Using the rag to protect her hand from the heat, she checked. No. Were the spark plug cables connected? She jiggled them. They felt fine. Wait a minute...

"You've got a broken battery cable," she called out.

Humph. She could replace the cable, but she didn't have one handy. She walked back to Imogene's window, mentally running through the contents of her Volare. Which would be...well, everything she owned. But what did she have that was useful and easily accessible?

"I'm kind of ashamed to admit this," Imogene said, "but I don't know how serious a problem that is. Before my husband died three years ago, I didn't even know how to put gas in the car."

Cara kept her expression neutral. That explained the woman's skepticism about Cara's car-repair skills. "A broken battery cable isn't too serious." She hesitated. "You know how to fill your tank now, right?"

"I sure do," Imogene said. "I've learned a lot since Harold died. And I got elected."

"Then I'd say you've been very resilient."

"Thank you." The older woman sat up taller. "It took me a while."

"That's understandable after such a loss," Cara said. Emotional trauma was hard to get past. She should know. But she had a plan for her own resilience, a plan that included moving to Abundance, a town she'd never heard of before last week and picked solely because of its name. Surely things would *have* to be better in a place called Abundance. With a new town, a new look, and a new name, she could start over and find what she so desperately wanted—a community, possibly even one day a family, to make her feel valued and loved.

But first, this repair job. "Is that your briefcase?" She pointed to the seat beside Imogene.

"Ye-es," Imogene said, sounding as if she now had more doubts about Cara's roadside assistance.

"Sorry, dumb question." What else could the big black case be? "What I mean is, do you have any binder clips in there?"

A grin spread across Imogene's face. "What size do you need?"

Two minutes later, Cara yelled out from under the hood. "Try it now."

Imogene cranked the engine, and it roared to life.

Cara hooked her thumbs in her shorts pockets and gave the engine a nod of approval. She'd done it! Who said a woman couldn't have a little mechanical know-how? She used the rag to protect her fingers as she lowered the sunbaked hood, then went to talk to Imogene.

"I can't believe you fixed it," Imogene said with a note of respect. "With office supplies."

"It might hold quite a while, but you should get a new cable as soon as you can. How about I follow you into town just in case? I'm headed there anyway to pick up the key to my apartment."

Imogene's head angled to one side. "Are you new to Abundance?"

"I am. I'm moving in today, and tomorrow I begin looking for a job."

"What do you do? Maybe I can help."

"Usually accounting, but I'd take any office position.

I'm a decent typist." She was also skilled at dodging reporters, but there was no need to mention that. "And I'm rather good at dealing with copiers that act up."

"I bet you are." Imogene looked Cara up and down. "I've been having a terrible time hiring a new secretary. Why don't you come in tomorrow for an interview?"

The air whooshed out of Cara's lungs. A possible job, just because she'd stopped to help? "Really? That would be great."

"Nine o'clock." Imogene reached out the window and gave Cara a firm handshake. "This may work out well. You're clearly bright, and if you can do battle with that copier the way you dealt with this car, all of city hall will thank me. Let me give you directions to my office."

Will Hamlin glanced from the highway to the notebook on the passenger seat of his Toyota pickup. He'd had an excellent interview with Alice Butler, a retired school-bus driver. That interview would make a solid feature story, the type of feature that he, as the new editor, wanted more of in *The Abundance News*.

Of course, Alice hadn't thought Abundance needed to know how she quietly helped the homebound elderly, but Will did. Once he mentioned that a story about her kindness might inspire someone else to think of others, she'd agreed to the interview.

Each week, Alice stopped by the homes of thirteen people, each too old or frail to drive, each of whom lived alone. She visited, she said, to make sure their glasses were clean. "Folks who are far-sighted can't see very well when they take their glasses off to wash them, but I can see every one of those spots."

But Alice did more than merely polish the glasses of the people she visited. She asked about their health, made sure their prescriptions were filled, and checked that food was in the fridge. Most importantly, for many of the people she visited, Alice was the only person they saw each week.

It wasn't a job. She wasn't paid by the county or the state or the federal government. She did it because she hoped someone would do the same for her when she was older. "And," she said, "because it's the Christian thing to do."

The humility of the woman, the basic goodness—that was what Will wanted to capture in his article.

Once he got back to the paper, he'd do his best. Then he would go home, take off his tie, and change out of his dress shirt and pants and into some gym shorts. He would have a nice, quiet evening with no meeting to cover. He might even take his TV dinner out on his back deck. He was actually supposed to have Mondays off since he worked every Saturday getting out both the Saturday and Sunday editions. Being promoted from reporter to editor hadn't meant much of a shift in his job duties, just the addition of more.

But what was going on up ahead?

Two cars sat at the side of the road, a green Lincoln Continental with an Abundance Lions Club bumper sticker and a white Volare. The Volare was unfamiliar and probably belonged to that redheaded woman. But the Lincoln? That belonged to Imogene Findley, the mayor who was furious with him.

Had they been in a wreck? He couldn't tell from here. Whatever was going on, it appeared Imogene was in trouble. Will pulled up behind her car and climbed out. He might be able to help her and by doing so get back in her good graces. She was an important news source. He needed her to take his calls. And besides, most of the time they got along well. After all, they both loved Abundance.

He looked more closely at the redhead. Mid-twenties. Wearing tan shorts and a pale blue T-shirt. Evidently, she was someone passing through. Any girl that cute in his hometown, he would have noticed.

He walked over to where she stood by Imogene's window.

Imogene's granddaughters waved frantically from the backseat as if they were afraid he might not notice them.

He bent down and peeked in. "Hey, girls. Nice blue hair ribbons, Joanna. And Jennifer, I like your purple ones."

Jennifer patted her pigtails, and Joanna's eyes sparkled.

He stood back up and looked at Imogene and the redhead. "Hi, Imogene. And—"

"If it isn't Will Hamlin, my least favorite person." Imogene held out a hand toward the redhead. "Will, meet Cara Smith. She's just moving to Abundance."

"Nice to meet you," he said. He shot a look at Imogene. Not the most gracious introduction he'd ever had.

"Pleased to meet you too." Cara reached to shake his hand but stopped. She wiped her fingers on a rag she held, then waved and tucked her hands behind her.

Up close, she looked even prettier. Her eyes were a pale greenish-blue, the sort of eyes a man might drown in, like the sea by some Mediterranean island.

And she was moving to Abundance? Wow. Lately, it seemed women his age only wanted to leave.

"Will's the editor of the local paper, *The Abundance News*," Imogene said to Cara. "A publication that doesn't always quote people correctly. Something to remember if you work with him professionally."

Cara's shoulders stiffened, and she took a half step back.

Heat flared in Will's chest. "Imogene, you know that misquote was in an article written by your niece, the same niece you asked me to hire as an intern this summer."

"Who I expect you to be training up better than that. I've been working for months to bring that manufacturer to Abundance. Cyndi's article may have blown our chance. The community needs those jobs."

"I'm having her personally mail them a copy of the retraction," Will said. "There's not much more I can do."

Imogene's mouth pinched up.

He shrugged. He was trying his best as editor, although some days he wondered if, at thirty, he was ready for the challenge. Obviously, Cyndi hadn't been ready for hers. He'd given her a chance with that big story, but she'd gotten the main quote of the piece all wrong. Unfortunately, he had no way of knowing until after the story ran, when the source called to complain. For now, she was back to writing the police reports, community calendar, and obits. "Anyway, I saw you two on the side of the road here. Do you need help?"

"Can you fix a broken battery cable?" Imogene's voice had a condescending note.

"Well, no." To be honest, he didn't know how to fix anything. Except a run-on sentence. "But I can offer you a ride to town."

"Not necessary," Imogene said. "Cara fixed it. No need to assume we're helpless just because we're female."

Will tugged at his collar. He hadn't made any such assumption. "I was simply trying to help."

The two women looked at him with the same expression, like royalty dismissing riffraff.

He turned and walked back to his truck. If he'd had any sense, he'd have driven by and stayed in the air conditioning.

Stopping had been a waste of time, time he should have spent on his feature.

And clearly, he'd never have a shot with that cute redhead. The mayor had already convinced her that he was an irresponsible journalist and sexist to boot.

Thanks a lot, Imogene.

Chapter Two

"Will, you have to do something about Kirk." Velma strode into Will's office, uninvited, parked herself by the fax machine, and planted her hands on her hips. Tall and angular, with graying hair and a pointy chin, the features editor of *The Abundance News* often reminded Will of a great blue heron.

He folded his copy of the day's paper, fresh off the presses. From the basement, he heard the reassuring hum of the machines, cranking out more. Was it too much to ask to have five minutes to sit and enjoy the smell of fresh ink and congratulate himself for one more issue sent to press on time?

From the way Velma's lips tightened, apparently so.

"Kirk's desk is an absolute sty," she said. "Papers keep spilling onto my desk, not to mention how unprofessional it looks. Plus the stink from his gym bag is enough to make me ill. I'm surprised you can't smell it in here."

Will laid the Tuesday edition of the newspaper by his Rolodex. This must be what parenting was like with bratty kids who enjoyed tattling on each other.

He had two letters to the editor to read and an editorial to pound out. More importantly, it was time for lunch. But instead of grabbing a big, juicy burger, he had to deal with a sports editor who should leave his gym bag in his car and with Velma, the clean desk queen. He didn't want to know her opinion of the piles of paper in his office.

Will rose to his feet. Best to get her back in the newsroom before she told him. "Show me the problem."

They walked out of his office, and she spread her hands out like a hostess displaying a prize on a game show.

The newsroom seemed the same as always. Dark green carpeting, dingy gray walls, and fluorescent lights that hung from a dropped acoustical tile ceiling with stains in the corner where the bathroom sink upstairs in advertising had leaked. A large window looked out on the dry cleaners across Ninth Street.

Near the front door, Kim, the receptionist, sat behind the counter answering yet another call from someone asking what was showing at the movie theater tonight. Frankly, if the people of Abundance wanted to know what the theater's ad said, they should buy a copy of the paper.

In the central part of the room, the official newsroom space, the four reporters' desks—each with an electric typewriter—were shoved together in a rectangle. Kirk and Velma had the prize spots near the wall where they each had a bulletin board. Velma's board was divided into six equally sized sections, with one piece of paper centered in each. Kirk's board held a wall calendar and a hodgepodge of papers at all angles. Which was somewhat the same arrangement as his hair.

Yes, Kirk's desk was a mess, with papers piled into a perimeter wall. And yes, his gym bag was tossed on the floor beside his chair. Will didn't smell anything unusual though. The newsroom smelled like it always did, of greasy food from Cassidy's Diner and warm wax from the machines in the back shop that coated the typeset copy so it would stick to the layout pages.

Will examined the other two desks.

Russell, the news reporter, had the one next to Kirk, closest to the back shop and Will's office. His chair was empty.

Cyndi, their intern for the summer, sat at her desk in front of the window, typing awkwardly.

Will leaned into Velma. "Did she hurt her hands?" he asked.

"I was upstairs checking something in a back issue, but I'd say she just painted her nails," Velma whispered. "They weren't that coral color when she came in this morning."

Will crossed his arms over his chest. Then, yep, everything in the newsroom was all too familiar.

Sometimes it seemed that working at *The Abundance News* had been nicer when Cyndi's desk had been his. When he'd been the senior reporter. When Russell had been his buddy, and Hal had been the editor. But Hal had retired, and Dad had promoted Will to editor, a position with double the stress and a diminutive bump in pay. Will had a suspicion that Hal's salary had been twenty-five percent more than his.

The door to the street opened, and Dad came in,

carrying a Styrofoam cup from Cassidy's. "Hey, Will, have you got a minute?"

"We can discuss this later," Velma said and hurried to her desk.

"Good to see you, Dad." Will waved a hand toward his office. "C'mon in."

Dad walked in, waited until Will followed him, and shut the door. He must have met someone for an early lunch. In the summer Dad almost always wore jeans and a T-shirt, not dress pants and a tie.

"Son, we need to talk."

The tone of his voice made Will's muscles tense. "Is everyone okay?" he said. "Mom—?"

"Everyone's fine. It's the paper."

Will sank into his chair. Both Mom and Dad owned the *News*, which had been started by Mom's father, but Dad was the publisher. Mostly, he left business decisions to the general manager, but lately he'd been stopping by to talk to Will about the bottom line. He probably wanted to explain again how news coverage affected circulation. Although Will wasn't the math whiz his dad was, he already knew that.

Dad sat in the chair across the desk, took a sip from his cup, and pushed up his plastic-framed glasses. "I may have to sell the *News*."

Will's muscles tightened. "What?"

"I hate to even consider it, but you know Mom and I have been struggling since we took out that second mortgage to buy those extra sixty acres." Embarrassment flickered through Dad's eyes. "Don't worry. I'd insist whoever buys it keeps you on as editor for a year."

Will planted his feet and leaned forward, one hand on his desk. "Dad—"

"Subscription revenue is at a real low. Combined with a slight dip in advertising, it's enough to mean we're going into the red. And the folks up in advertising say without more subscribers, they can't sell more ads."

"I've only been the editor here for four months." Will held up four fingers. Four measly months. Dad wasn't even giving him a chance.

"Each month, subscriptions have slipped. I'd like to give you more time, but finances being what they are… Besides, you're not pursuing the stories that draw readers. Even after our talk a few weeks ago." Dad's brow lowered. "I just saw Russell at Cassidy's, having lunch with that young new schoolteacher."

Will's chest grew hot. He'd thought Russell was out working on a story.

"He asked if I'd talk with you about his article on the mowing contract for the junior high, to see if I can convince you to run it."

"That article could get us sued."

"But a contract awarded without a fair bidding process? That's news. That's what will get our readership up and let us charge more for advertising."

"I told Russell I'd run it if he got two sources willing to go on record. Hal would have insisted on the same thing."

"Even so, Hal made sure the *News* was breaking stories."

Will blew out a loud breath. Dad didn't even trust him to handle editorial decisions. "No chain is going to cover the news properly in this town. They'll fill the pages with wire copy and cut staff." Not that Dad hadn't already done that to some extent, insisting Will wait to hire his own replacement and limp by with an intern for the summer.

"You're not covering local news so well yourself if you're sitting on stories like Russell's." Dad stood. "I promise I'll try to find a decent chain to buy it."

"Shouldn't you be talking to Veronica up in advertising and the folks in circulation?" Will said, unable to keep the anger out of his voice.

Dad held out a hand to block Will's argument. "I'm going to tell them the same thing. I'm giving you all two months to show a profit—or simply break even. I just can't afford for the paper to lose money." He gave an awkward wave, walked out, and shut the door behind him.

Will slumped down in his chair and stared blankly at the bookshelf across from his desk. There, between two of his textbooks from school, was his dog-eared copy of *All the President's Men*, the book that had inspired him to go into journalism after his failed stint in the Army. How could someone read about Bob Woodward and Carl Bernstein digging out the truth about Nixon and *not* want to fight for truth? Not want to uncover big news? But here in Abundance, he didn't know any big news, except for that cute redhead moving to town. And he didn't want the paper to run a story like Russell's, with vague references and accusations. A story like that could ruin someone's life with a lie. As Will knew from personal experience, passing on a lie could lead to an endless stream of guilt.

He hadn't been a reporter when he'd done it, but he sure had ruined someone's life. In the worst possible way. Back in high school, he'd overheard that his best friend

Gary's girlfriend was cheating on him. He'd told Gary, as kindly as he could. Two hours later, Gary was dead, his car smashed into a tree in what Will would always believe was suicide. He'd tried to talk to Gary's parents, to tell them what he'd done, but Gary's dad had said the accident was too painful for them to discuss.

Will couldn't bring himself to tell anyone else. Which left him with a lifetime of secret guilt.

Especially when he learned that the rumor about Gary's girlfriend wasn't true.

So yeah, he was cautious with rumors. He certainly wasn't printing them in the newspaper. That was no way to make up for what he'd done in high school.

But he did believe in helping the community. And he did need a story.

Not just any story, but one that would bring in new subscribers, possibly even win an award to put up in the newsroom. An award that—if Dad didn't sell the paper first—would remind him that *The Abundance News* needed to remain privately owned.

Somehow, Will would find that story.

First, though, he needed to act like he was in charge. He got up, straightened his tie, and went into the newsroom. "Kirk, Velma, I want you each to scoot your desk back about six inches."

Kirk peered over his wall of paper. "And have a gap between them?"

"Exactly," Will said. Maybe the sports editor would be more concerned about the mess if he had to pick up papers that fell onto the floor. "And Cyndi, quit goofing off. Get over to the police station and write down the information from today's blotter."

Cyndi angled her head in a manner that held more insolence than guilt. After a second, though, she pushed back her frizzy hair and pulled a notepad and pen from the drawer.

Will headed out the door toward Cassidy's. He'd get a burger to take back to his office, and he'd tell Russell that if he wanted his story on the junior high school mowing bids to run, he needed to corroborate his facts, not take a two-hour lunch, and not go over Will's head.

Then Will would figure out how to attract more readers. Because, one way or another, he had to convince Dad not to sell the *News*.

"Cara, if you can get that letter typed up and let me sign it, I'd like it to go out today." Imogene picked up a thick, stapled stack of papers on her desk. "And I'll try to get through this report from the street department."

"I'll get right on it." Cara grabbed her notebook and went back to the outer office, closing Imogene's door as she exited.

So far for her first day on the job, the position in the mayor's office was working out fine. Of course, there were a few problems. She shot a look at the file cabinets, a horror story of disorganization. But they were problems she could handle.

She couldn't believe yesterday's job interview with Imogene had gone so easily. Cara had worried about her references, all from back in college, but the mayor had barely glanced at them. She'd been more interested in how

Cara would handle irate callers and how well she typed. Cara wasn't the fastest, but thanks to a persnickety high school teacher, accuracy would be no problem, especially on that fancy IBM Selectric.

As for her new apartment, between the appliances and the upholstery, there was enough avocado green to resemble the inside of a guacamole factory. Still, the place was furnished, clean, and comfortable. Except for her winter clothes, which were still in her laundry basket in the back seat of her car, she'd moved in all her stuff.

Yesterday she'd even walked up and down Main Street, opened an account at the bank, and found a diner that would be handy for lunches. And she'd been thoroughly charmed by downtown Abundance. The maple trees planted at irregular intervals in circles in the sidewalk. The big pink ad painted on the side of a brick building for Miss Millie's Dance School. *Just Up These Stairs*, it read, with a bold arrow pointing to a side entrance. The red-white-and-blue fire hydrants that must have been painted in 1976. And the plump orange cat that slept on a cushion on the inside windowsill of the hardware store. Abundance seemed like a town that lived at a slower pace, with no apologies. All in all, a place she could like.

Now she settled into the chair at her desk where she sat at a right angle to the hall.

To her left, a door led to Imogene's office. To her right, file cabinets flanked the entrance to the hall. Behind her, a connecting door led to the treasurer's outer office. And across the room, sunbeams filtered in two tall windows onto the maroon-and-white tile floor.

The mayor's suite was in the corner on the second floor

of city hall, a building erected about 1900. The whole place had a sturdy unpretentiousness that somehow made Cara believe that decade after decade, people had come here, done their honest best to serve the community, and gone home proud of their work. Exactly what she wanted, the opportunity to contribute and feel that she had value.

Perhaps if she had looked longer and found a position in accounting, she might be making more money. For now, though, a job unrelated to accounting was perfect.

If she wanted to do well here, she should start by getting Imogene's letter out. She turned to her typewriter.

"Cara?" An assistant to the city treasurer came through the connecting door to the treasurer's office. The woman was somewhere in her forties. She wore sensible, low, navy pumps and a baby blue pantsuit that must have been in her closet for several years, given the width of the collar. Her hair was dark brown, a brown that was—from what Cara knew of Miss Clairol—one shade too dark for coloring her gray.

Not that Cara wanted anyone to focus too closely on clothes or hair color. She'd done her best, dying her blond hair red, but she worried about her light brown eyebrows. Not quite enough though, to put hair color on them. What if that stuff dripped into her eyes?

And as for clothes, with luck, no one would notice that her outfits weren't knockoffs of designer labels but were the real deal. And probably, most workers in the Abundance City Hall didn't carry butter-soft leather handbags that retailed for four hundred dollars. She'd sold her luxury car without a thought, but she hadn't been able to bring herself to give up that purse.

But what was this woman's name? It wasn't Rachel. That was the quiet part-time employee in the treasurer's office. No, this woman was one of the first people Cara had met, and she had that "God Answers Prayer" sign on her desk, but... "I'm sorry," Cara said. "I've forgotten your—"

"DeeDee McAlister." The woman tapped her fingers to her chest. "No need to apologize. I'm sure Imogene introduced you to every person in the building. How are things going so far?"

"Not too bad." Cara didn't need to admit that she had yet to figure out the filing system.

"Imogene said you recently moved to town?"

"Two days ago. I sure do like Abundance. Such a lovely place." She picked up her notes for the letter Imogene wanted.

"It *is* a lovely town." DeeDee's tone held pride and a note of approval of Cara's opinion. "Where are you living?"

"An apartment over on Pine Street. The complex is called Fairview."

"I had a friend who lived there. My husband and I have a farmhouse out west of town." DeeDee took a step closer to Cara's desk. "So where did you move from?"

Cara's stomach twitched. "S-Southern Illinois."

"Oh?" DeeDee sounded more interested. "What town?"

Cara's mouth grew dry, and she rolled her chair back ever-so-slightly away from DeeDee. The woman asked a good question. A very good question. One Cara should have been prepared for. And she would have except that this whole lying business bothered her so much. "Uh..."

"Is it true?" A heavyset, older woman with poufy gold hair popped in from the hall. The city treasurer, the woman Imogene said was such a sweetheart.

"Is what true, Francine?" DeeDee said.

"Cara, can you fix the copy machine?" Francine said. "Some light is flashing, and I need a copy made immediately."

Cara got to her feet. "No guarantees, but I'd be happy to try." Not just happy but delighted as it meant the conversation with DeeDee was over.

She'd deal with the copier, then get Imogene's letter out.

And before she talked to DeeDee again, she'd figure out where in Illinois she had supposedly lived. Because she was not letting anyone near the truth about her past. This was a good place, with good people. She could make a decent life here.

If only she could keep her real identity a secret.

Chapter Three

Four out of five.

Cara had moved into her new apartment on Monday. Now, only three days later, four of the five bulbs in her bathroom had already burned out. Most Missouri caves offered better lighting for applying makeup.

But, thanks to the fact that Abundance had a hardware store downtown, she'd been able to start her lunch hour by buying new light bulbs. She still had plenty of time to pick up her club sandwich and get back to her desk.

She switched the bag with light bulbs to her other hand, pulled open the door to Cassidy's Diner, and went to the counter, inhaling deeply. The whole restaurant smelled delicious, like fried onions and bacon. At a counter with a thick gray edge, all the stools were taken but one, and every red vinyl booth was full. If the diner was this crowded at lunch on a Thursday, the food had to be good.

Cara stood behind the only empty stool, right under a

perfectly placed air-conditioning vent. Today was already a scorcher. For a moment, she closed her eyes and enjoyed the cool air.

"Are you here for a carryout order?" the waitress said.

"Yes, for Cara."

"It's not up yet, but I poured your Cherry Coke." The waitress slid a Styrofoam cup in front of Cara.

"Thanks." Cara sat, unwrapped her straw, and took a long drink.

There was a brief lull in the conversations around her, filled only with the radio playing Kenny Rogers' "The Gambler."

The waitress angled her head to the left. "I'll be right back." She turned to look down the counter. "Don't worry, Will. I'll get you that last piece of peanut butter pie."

Cara's shoulders tensed, and she gave a furtive glance to the side.

Two stools over, past a man in a muddy-brown sports coat, sat the guy she'd met outside town, the journalist Imogene had warned her about.

As if Cara needed the advice. A woman couldn't have her family disgraced in the newspapers and harassed by TV reporters and not know to steer clear of journalists.

She needed to pay for her lunch and leave.

But the little shelf below the window to the kitchen, the place where she imagined her lunch would appear, was empty.

Fine. She would sit here and enjoy her fountain Cherry Coke. In all probability, the guy wouldn't even notice her anyway.

The man in the sports coat bumped her elbow as he got

up. He mumbled an apology and walked away.

Cara took another drink and studied a sign behind the counter that read "Today's Homemade Pies: Peanut Butter Cream, Gooseberry, Lemon Meringue." She wasn't planning to have pie, but she was not looking toward that journalist, even if he was kind of cute. Give a reporter even the slightest hint of vulnerability, and—

"Hi. Remember me?" He moved to the stool beside her. "I'm Will."

Cara pressed her teeth together and drew in a breath. "Uh, yeah. Hi." She gave him a quick once-over, taking in his gray-and-white-striped button-down, navy pants, and slightly crooked tie. Then she resumed her study of the pie menu.

"It's a terrible place to be in."

Huh? She looked back at him. Okay, he was more than "kind of" cute with his wavy brown hair and hazel eyes and that streak of ketchup on his chin, but he didn't make sense. "What's a terrible place?"

"Trying to decide. Usually, I can get it down to two choices, like today I ruled out lemon meringue. Cassidy's serves that year-round. But gooseberry's only offered in the summer, and peanut butter cream isn't on the rotation that often."

"Oh." She had no interest in talking to the man, but he seemed harmless, rambling on about pie and oblivious to the ketchup. She rubbed her chin with an exaggerated movement hoping to get the message across.

"Since you're new here," he said. "I'll let you in on a town secret."

"That's all right." The last thing—the absolute last

thing—she needed was a conversation with someone who wanted to share secrets.

"Outsiders don't know it." Will continued as if she hadn't even spoken, and he hadn't gotten the hint about the ketchup. "But the best pie here at Cassidy's is apple. You'd think it would be boring, the same as apple pie anywhere, but they do something different with the filling. And if you get it with ice cream? Best dessert on earth."

She rubbed her chin once more.

No response.

At last, she couldn't stand it. "You have ketchup on your chin," she blurted out.

Will froze for a second, and his ears turned pink, then he wiped the ketchup away. "Gone?"

"Yes," Cara said. Now if her food would hurry up and arrive, she could leave while he ate his pie.

"Here you go." The waitress set a bag in front of Cara, handed a Styrofoam container to Will, and tore two tickets off her pad.

"Give me her bill as well," Will said to the waitress.

"You don't need to do that." Cara shot up from the stool. "Really."

"I insist. You saved me from walking through downtown looking like an idiot."

"All right," she said slowly. "Thank you." She slid her purse on her shoulder, picked up her light bulbs, and then stopped. "Oops. Almost forgot my pop."

She shifted her bags to one hand and grabbed the cup.

Will pulled a twenty out of his wallet, handed it to the waitress, then turned back to Cara. "Besides, you might find a body buried in the basement of city hall and give me the scoop. I'm desperate for a story."

Even though the AC over Cara's stool had kicked off, a shiver ran through her. She should have known. Reporters were always hunting for dirt.

"C'mon. I'll walk you back." Will pocketed his change and held open the diner door.

She did not need an escort, especially not from a snoopy reporter. "I'm sure you'd like to get back to your office and eat your pie," she said.

"The paper's one block past city hall. The fastest way to my office goes right by where you're headed."

"Well, okay." Cara tried to smile politely. After all, he had bought her lunch. If she kept acting nervous, it would only make him suspicious. And there was a chance she was being paranoid.

"Let's cross here," he said at the corner by the bank. "So we can be in the shade." He pointed across the street to three shops in a row with awnings.

She couldn't argue with that, not with the heat coming off the ground in waves.

"I bet we'll see each other a lot," he said once they reached the other side of the street. "I eat lunch at Cassidy's almost every day. Usually a little past twelve though. I can't leave until the paper goes to press." His eyes twinkled. "By that time I'm starving, definitely in need of lunch, including pie."

Cara gave a noncommittal shrug. Maybe she could trade with DeeDee and take the earlier lunch. She did not need to be running into a reporter every day.

"So I heard you're from Illinois. Are you settling into Abundance okay?"

"I am," she said, trying to sound casual, despite her inner panic at his reference to her past. "Everything's going great. Except for my light bulbs." She raised the hand with the bags. "I had to buy new ones. Most of the ones in my apartments seemed to burn out as soon as I moved in."

"Isn't that the way it always goes?" Will said. "Is—?"

"So you're the editor of the paper?" Cara interrupted. If she got this guy talking about himself, he wouldn't be asking questions about her life. "Name on the door and everything?"

"Well, no. The former editor, Hal, never had his name there, and he was in charge for ages. I've only had the job for four months. Putting my name on the door...wouldn't sit well with the staff."

"Ahh," Cara said. "Trying to step into extra-large shoes can be difficult."

"Yeah." Some of the carefree gleam faded from Will's eyes. "Even more difficult when—no matter how hard you work—you got the job because your dad's the publisher."

Cara looked at him more closely and pressed her lips together to keep from telling him that she'd been in a similar situation when her dad hired her. "I, um, I imagine that makes it twice as hard to prove yourself."

Will let out a long breath, and his gaze caught hers. "Most people don't get that. And it's not the woman who's worked there since I was a little kid. It's the guy who's my age."

"I know," Cara said. "I mean, it makes sense," she corrected, her muscles suddenly twitchy. "But it will get better." At least it did for her. For a while.

"I hope so," Will said.

She turned toward the alley to the back parking lot for city hall. "Well, thanks for buying my lunch. I'm just going to put my light bulbs in my car." Hopefully, he would head on down the block.

"Sure." Will stayed in step with her, once again not getting her hint. "I'll point out the paper for you, in case you ever want to stop by for a tour. It's pretty cool to see the presses run."

Not an offer she'd be taking him up on, no matter how much she empathized with his work situation. But sure enough, once they were in the parking lot, she saw the top of the two-story building with a sign that read "*The Abundance News.*" From a business perspective, it did make sense for the newspaper to be right near city hall, but part of her wished it was five miles outside town.

Another part of her... Well, despite his talk about needing a big story, Will hadn't seemed nosy. Hadn't asked a lot of questions about where she'd moved from or anything. He seemed more focused on adjusting to his new role as editor. And on the day she came to town, he'd been kind enough to stop to help Imogene. Plus somewhere along the line, he'd figured out how to tell those twins apart. Even took the time to talk to them. All in all, he seemed like a nice person.

Nice, like DeeDee. Exactly the type of people she wanted to meet in her new town. Was it really so awful that the newspaper was close? That she might see him occasionally? If she let him, he might turn out to be a friend.

"Thanks again for lunch," she said as they came to her car in the back of the lot.

"You're welcome," he said. "Allow me." He reached across to open the car door, and his arm brushed hers.

An awareness of how close his body was shot through her. Was it the connection she'd sensed when they talked about work? The way his ears had turned pink when she pointed out the ketchup? Or was she just lonely, being new in town? Whatever it was, she needed to be careful.

She tried to arrange her face into a nothing-happened expression.

But Will's gaze narrowed on her as if he'd felt it too.

For a second they both stood there. Awkward. Uncertain. As if any movement might intensify the feeling. And—no matter how much she suddenly wanted to—she couldn't go there.

Hurriedly she put her light bulbs on the front passenger seat. Not a big production, but the everyday nature of the action was enough to break the tension.

Will shut the door, and the two of them walked to the back of the car. He half turned toward the paper, then chuckled. "Hey, great bumper sticker." He tipped his head toward the rear of her Volare.

The final knots in her muscles eased. "Isn't it hilarious?" she said. The used car had come with a bumper sticker for Erlene's Bait and Pizza. Certainly, a much better topic to discuss than that...whatever that feeling was that had passed between them. She didn't see how, with no address or phone number, he could possibly connect the bumper sticker to a town in Kansas.

"Pretty funny," he said with a laugh. "It makes you think they might offer worms as a pizza topping." He gave a brief wave and headed across the parking lot.

Cara opened the back door of city hall, and as she started up the stairs to the second floor, her doubts flooded back. What was she thinking? Will Hamlin was the worst possible person for her to befriend in Abundance. Not only was he a reporter, but he was so cute and nice and easy to talk to. If she wasn't careful, she'd fall for him, let down her guard, and tell him everything.

And that simply couldn't happen.

Will pulled a plastic fork out of his desk drawer, popped open the Styrofoam container, and took a bite of peanut butter cream pie.

Excellent. Perfect flavor, perfect crust, just as he'd expected.

But Cara, the mayor's new secretary? The girl who, according to his friend in the street department, had said she was from *southern* Illinois? Not what he'd expected.

And unless his gut was off, not from southern Illinois.

First, she'd called her Coke a "pop." He'd never met anyone from around St. Louis who said *pop*. They all fell on the *soda* side of the line that seemed to bisect Missouri from north to south. He might not have remembered her word choice, or he might have assumed her parents were from Kansas City and were *pop* people if it weren't for the other clue, that bumper sticker.

Because Will had eaten at Erlene's Bait and Pizza when he visited his buddy Andy from journalism school. Once Will had seen for himself that the place wasn't a health hazard, that the bait shop was clearly divided from the restaurant, he'd had three slices of better-than-average pepperoni. And he hadn't been in Illinois. He'd been on the shores of Spotts Lake, in Spottsville, Kansas. A pleasant enough place, but unless they knew someone there like he did, not an area tourists would visit. Most likely, if someone had a bumper sticker for Erlene's, they were local.

He adjusted his chair and forked another bite of pie, careful to get the perfect ratio of whipped cream to peanut butter filling.

Cara's car had Missouri plates. Had those been on the vehicle when he met her at the side of the road? He wasn't sure.

Some observant reporter he was. She seemed like a nice enough girl, but if she wasn't, if her lie was connected to a big story, he'd missed a vital clue.

Probably it wouldn't amount to anything. But he was curious.

Tonight, after the long distance rates dropped, he'd give Andy a call and do some investigating. Because his gut was telling him that Cara Smith was definitely hiding something.

Chapter Four

Cara shoved the bottom file drawer closed with a resounding clank. Done. With five minutes left in the day. Now she could drive to a store in Columbia to buy storage boxes that would fit under her bed. Then she could move her winter clothes, which would never squeeze into her tiny closet, out of her backseat.

"What have you been doing over here all day?" DeeDee said from the door to the treasurer's office.

"Reorganizing the filing system," Cara said. "It was a disaster."

A look that might have been agreement passed through DeeDee's eyes.

But maybe it wasn't. "I hope the previous secretary wasn't a friend of yours," Cara added. "I don't mean to be rude by criticizing her system."

"No need to worry about that. She kind of thought she was above me." DeeDee's voice held an airy note as if the woman's judgment hadn't troubled her. "Like she thought my love of *Dallas* was silly."

"The TV show?"

"I never miss an episode. And this year I recorded them all on my new Betamax."

"I love *Dallas*," Cara said. "It's absolutely the best show on TV."

"You sound like my daughter." DeeDee gave a wide smile. "You should come over some night and we can re-watch the final episode of the season."

"I'd love that," Cara said.

"Me too. Good job with those files." DeeDee waved and stepped back toward the treasurer's office.

"Thanks. Have a nice evening." Cara grabbed her purse, locked up, then hurried down the back stairs and stepped outside. Time to head to Columbia to get those storage boxes.

She'd finished her reorganization, found something in common with DeeDee, and now even the weather seemed to be cooperating. The parking lot was full of puddles, but the rain that had poured down for hours earlier in the day had stopped. A lovely evening for her drive. She really was settling in, getting the fresh start she'd dreamed of.

Cara unlocked her car and slid inside, then yelped. *What on earth?* She scrambled out.

The vinyl seats of her car were sopping wet. Near the sunroof, the fabric lining was ripped as if…as if the sunroof had leaked and water had built up inside the lining until it burst at the seam. The car seats and the carpeting and—she yanked open a rear door and checked the contents of her laundry basket—all her winter clothes were drenched. As was the backside of the pants she was wearing. She pulled the fabric away from her skin. The instant she let go, though, it stuck to her again.

Her muscles quivered as she slammed the rear door shut and glared at the dark clouds.

But it wasn't the clouds' fault. It was hers.

What had she been thinking, buying a used car from that slimy salesman back in Spottsville, especially a used car with a sunroof not installed by the manufacturer?

"I've got the perfect deal for you. A terrific vehicle we just took in," the salesman had said. "It's still in the service area, getting cleaned."

She'd noticed a weird vibe about him but—after she'd looked over the engine and taken the car for a test drive—she'd ignored that twist in her gut. She should have paid attention. The car was probably in the service area because it had leaked the last time it rained. Why fix it? Why not sell it to Baxter Smith's daughter?

Possibly, the car dealer would have sold the lemon to anyone. But with the way people had treated her back in Spottsville, she had to wonder if she'd been picked as a potential victim on purpose.

In an ideal world, fathers were supposed to love their children and provide for them. In her world? Dad had provided for her all right. He'd provided an entire town of people who hated her. But that's what happened when a man stole the life savings of unsuspecting retirees.

For all she knew, Dad had taken money from the elderly grandparents of that car salesman.

Queasiness rolled through her stomach, and she blew out a heavy breath.

Was she ever, ever going to escape her past? Ever truly be able to start over?

And what was she going to do with a car that was soaking wet?

Still not dry.

Will shoved his warm, damp jeans back inside the laundromat dryer, dug another quarter out of his pocket, and fed the machine. All the rest of his clothes were dry and back in his basket, just not his jeans.

He checked his watch and sat in the orange plastic chair across from the dryer.

In the back corner of the laundromat, the ten-year-old playing pinball let out a whoop, drowning out a song by Mac Davis on the radio. Will looked at the kid. Yep, most likely that boy's high score was Will's excitement for the evening.

The Abundance Wash 'n' Wear wasn't the most interesting place to spend a Friday night, but he'd put laundry off as long as possible. And unlike the last time he'd been here, when it really had been the "hottest place in town," the air conditioning was working. It hummed along without a wheeze, lowering the humidity. Definitely a plus.

Today had been a good day. Russell had gotten decent quotes for his story on the mowing contract, giving the piece some credibility, and Will had been able to run it. Granted, after they had all the facts, the mowing contract was only costing the taxpayers an extra fifty dollars, not enough to be considered breaking news. But in the future money would be spent more fairly. No more funneling jobs to someone's cousin.

Exactly the role *The Abundance News* should play, bringing issues to light so all would be run fairly. Sure, Will loved writing features, but his most important role was bringing unbiased information to the public so citizens could take action to make the community a better place. Which was why he'd tried to call his buddy Andy over in Kansas last night. If the mayor's new secretary was lying to people, Will wanted to figure out why. Even though Andy didn't live in Spottsville, he was in Wichita, only thirty miles away.

Andy hadn't been home, but Will had left a message with someone in the newsroom at the Wichita paper, asking Andy if he knew anything about a woman named Cara Smith. Because, seriously, how many places were named Erlene's Bait and Pizza? And—

He sat up in his chair. The very woman he'd been thinking of had just come in, carrying a mountain of laundry in a yellow plastic basket. Enough laundry to keep her here awhile, possibly long enough for Will to get some answers.

Cara glanced in his direction, then landed her basket with a thud on the first dryer, four down from his. He couldn't help but notice that the dress pants she was wearing had a damp spot on the back as if she'd fallen in a puddle. And her mascara was smeared as if she'd been crying.

"Hi, Cara." He walked toward her.

"Hi." She didn't sound happy. Good thing he hadn't mentioned the puddle.

He peered more closely at her laundry basket. The whole thing was filled with wet clothes. "Did the dryer in your apartment break?"

"I don't have a washer-dryer." Her voice quivered, and she avoided his eyes.

A man with good sense wouldn't ask any more questions, not with her voice all shaky like that. But Mom always said he had more curiosity than sense. "Then how did you get so much wet laundry? You didn't go to Beck's, did you? Their dryers break all the time."

"I've never even heard of Beck's." She looked around the laundromat. "Where's the machine that takes my dollars and gives me quarters?"

"It's back by the pinball game, but it's broken."

She pulled out her wallet, yanked back the zipper, and dumped the change compartment on top of the dryer. Pennies, two dimes, and a safety pin fell out. One penny rolled off the dryer and landed on the floor inside a chip in the linoleum. She scrunched her eyes closed. "I cannot believe this day," she said under her breath.

"Here." Will picked up the penny and held it out to her along with two quarters from his shorts pocket. "And..." He brought out three more quarters from his other pocket. From his experience at the Wash 'n' Wear, he'd say she'd need more than a dollar to get all those clothes dry.

Her eyes locked on the quarters. "You don't need them?"

"I'm good."

"Thanks." She handed him the dimes, five pennies, and a dollar bill, then took all five quarters.

Will sat in a chair halfway between their dryers. The

mom of the pinball wizard called her son over to carry one of her baskets of clean clothes, and the two of them trudged out of the laundromat, leaving Will and Cara alone.

Cara rapidly sorted her clothes, tossing most of them into the machine. Some clothes she returned to the basket wet.

At last, she collapsed into the chair next to him. "All right. I'll explain." Her words echoed in the nearly empty room, bouncing off the tile floor, and she continued more quietly. "This has to seem weird."

"It almost looks like you put your clothes in the basket and turned a hose on them."

"My sunroof leaked," she said. "I hadn't taken my winter clothes into my apartment because I hadn't figured out where to put them."

"And we got all that rain." Almost two inches today.

"Yeah. There's no place in my apartment to hang up this much stuff to dry."

He'd have thought that a woman like Cara, who knew how to repair a broken battery cable, would take care of a problem like a leaky sunroof when it was minor. But he didn't mention that. He might be too curious for his own good, but he wasn't flat-out stupid. "Some part just gave out?"

"I bet there were warning signs the last time it rained," Cara said. "But I only bought the car last week. No wonder it was cheap. I'm sure the dealer, though, would claim he never knew." She wiped at the mascara on her face, smearing it into an even larger smudge. "I'll have to drive it to a garage in the morning. It's going to take industrial-strength fans to dry out the seats."

Will studied her face, then glanced at the brown linoleum. Probably she was right about the car dealer, and to have her sunroof leak after the hassle of moving, well, no wonder she seemed beat down.

Beat down, but still beautiful.

Except for that black mascara mark, her fair skin looked almost velvety. He grabbed a still-warm washcloth out of his laundry basket, sat back down, and held it toward her.

Her forehead furrowed.

"Wipe under your left eye," he said.

She did, totally missing the streak.

"No, here." He leaned closer and ran a finger under her eye and out toward her temple, barely brushing her skin. Which felt even softer than it looked.

She wiped the smudge away.

"Got it," he said. "You helped me with the ketchup. Now we're even." Well, as even as they could be, considering his racing pulse and the fact that she seemed unfazed by his touch.

Cara looked down at the washcloth and wadded it up. Her posture deflated. "Great," she said. "I've been sitting here looking like a clown."

"Nope." Will took the washcloth and tossed it back in his basket. "Clowns aren't pretty."

"Oh," she said. Her voice was breathy, the word almost a laugh. The corners of her lips curved up, and her eyelashes fluttered down.

While her eyes were closed, he grasped a shred of his journalistic savvy and peered at her, laser-focused—not on those eyelashes or those soft-looking lips—but on who he sensed she was. On what his gut told him.

And his gut said she wasn't out to harm the mayor's office. She simply seemed like someone who was having a hard time. She might even be in witness protection, trying to hide her identity for a good reason. Or trying to get away from an ex-husband or boyfriend.

Most likely, dealers sold cars from all over the place, possibly even from other states. She really might be from Illinois. Maybe she'd never heard of Erlene's Bait and Pizza before she bought her car. And maybe her parents were from Kansas, and she'd grown up hearing Coke called *pop*. Should he ask her where she was from, to be sure?

No. He didn't need to badger her after what she'd been through today.

He glanced at the floor. His call to Andy suddenly seemed slimy, like something a reporter for a tabloid might do.

He wasn't that kind of reporter. He didn't write stories about politicians meeting with Bigfoot or movie stars having plastic surgery.

He'd gotten all tangled up in suspicion, hoping for a big exposé to impress Dad when what he actually needed was to show some decency and kindness.

"I know a good place to take your car for repair. They'll even give you a loaner," he said. "And I'll help you get your dry clothes home...if you want." He shifted his weight in the chair. He didn't want to be so helpful that he seemed weird. "I mean, you can't put them on your wet car seat or back in there." He pointed to the wet clothes in her basket.

"That would be great," she said. Gratitude rang in her words, and tension eased around her blue-green eyes.

A light, tingling sensation filled Will's chest. He leaned back in his chair, his shoulders resting easily against the molded plastic. So what if his big plans for the weekend had been doing laundry? The Wash 'n' Wear wasn't nearly as dull as he'd thought.

In fact, some of the most intriguing people did laundry on a Friday night.

Including an intriguing someone who Will planned to get to know a whole lot better.

Chapter Five

Time for the final phase of his plan to win Cara's trust. At least enough for her to agree to a date with him.

From the hallway, Will peeked into the mayor's outer office.

Cara wasn't at her desk, but he could hear her talking in Imogene's private office. Behind Cara's desk, the connecting door to the treasurer's outer office stood open.

He sped a few feet down the hall, past where Cara might look out and spot him, and entered the treasurer's office from its main door to the hall. He cleared his throat.

DeeDee gave a quick thumbs up.

His accomplice was ready.

He'd thought, after he talked with Cara at the laundromat last week, that she'd go out with him if he asked. Late Monday afternoon he'd run into her on the street and learned she'd just gotten a call that her sunroof was fixed. Tuesday morning, after he checked some numbers at city hall, he'd popped into her office to say hi. Both times she'd been polite, but walled off in a way that made it clear that an invitation to lunch would be rejected. As if the time they'd spent together doing laundry, which he'd thought ended up being rather fun, had never happened.

Thus, the plan. Because try as he might, he couldn't get the cute redhead out of his mind.

Late Tuesday afternoon, he'd snuck in and left a piece of Cassidy's peach pie on her desk. Yesterday, again undetected, a slice of banana cream. But only after he'd had to stand in the hall for fifteen minutes until Imogene called Cara in to discuss some report. And when he'd returned to the paper, Velma had been waiting, annoyed, wanting to talk about the photos for her story on a local weaver.

Really, when she had sixteen specific points of complaint for the staff photographer, she should talk to him herself.

Today, to make the final phase of the pie plan go more smoothly, Will had enlisted an accomplice. DeeDee, his former fifth-grade Sunday school teacher, was more than happy to oblige and said Cara wouldn't suspect a thing. Apparently, she and DeeDee had become friends, bonding over their shared love of *Dallas*.

Across the room, Francine Young came out of her office and handed DeeDee a file. Then she rolled her eyes at Will and shook her head as if she knew all about the plan and thought he was an idiot. Lovable, perhaps, but an idiot.

Exactly what he'd expect from someone who worked

with rows of numbers all day. Francine was the nicest woman in the world, but clearly, she didn't have a journalist's creative nature or sense of adventure.

Next door, he heard the creak of Cara's chair as she sat back at her desk. He caught DeeDee's eye, pointed toward the mayor's office, and slipped into the hall.

"Cara, help!" DeeDee's voice rang out. "I was changing the correcting tape on my typewriter, and it unraveled. I've got a terrible mess."

"Coming!" Cara called, her chair squeaking again as she got up.

Will counted to five and then—when he heard her walk through the connecting door between the two offices—he crept a few feet down the hall and entered her office through the main door. He placed the Styrofoam container with a slice of apple pie on her desk. He was so good at this sneakiness, he was surprised the CIA hadn't tried to recruit him.

Should he leave a short note? Was there time? He reached for the notebook in his shirt pocket and—

The phone on Cara's desk rang.

Will froze, then dashed toward the hall.

Cara's voice sounded behind him. "Hold it right there, mister."

Busted. Slowly, he turned to face her.

"Hello?" she said into the phone.

He moved an inch toward the hallway, trying not to look at her. A good operative would not stand here thinking how the subject's green sweater hugged her curves in all the right places and made her eyes look mesmerizing. He would escape. Will slid another inch.

Cara glared at him.

He slumped against the wall. Some spy he was.

She transferred the call to Imogene, strode toward him, and crossed her arms over her sweater in a stance that claimed annoyance. Her eyes, though, held amusement. "More pie?"

"Yep."

"What flavor is it today?"

"Apple." He gave a sheepish grin. "I figured you'd guess it was from me and then, if I called, you might agree to have lunch with me." He hoped.

She pursed her lips and gazed toward the ceiling in an overly exaggerated expression of contemplation.

"So what do you say? Lunch at the diner today?" Why did he sound as nervous as if he was fifteen? "I, um, I could come by to walk you over at twelve-thirty."

"Well..." She dragged the word out like a form of torture.

He raised his eyebrows in an expression he hoped was endearing.

"All right," she said sweetly.

Adrenaline hummed through his veins. *Cool. Got to play it cool.* "Great. I'll see you then," he said in his best nonchalant, CIA tone.

Excellent. Even if things hadn't gone exactly as he'd hoped, the plan had worked.

Never before had he had to try so hard to get a first date with a girl. Certainly, he'd never had to sweeten anyone else up with pie.

But he had a feeling she was worth the effort.

Looks were often the first thing he noticed about a

woman. And Cara was no exception.

But it wasn't just her looks.

Cara Smith was someone special.

Cara reached across her desk and gave the container that held her apple pie a quick pat.

Ten more minutes and Will should be here to take her to lunch. She'd tried, after that evening at the laundromat, to convince herself she wanted nothing to do with him. He was a reporter after all. Even if he seemed harmless, he was the last person in town she should be spending time with.

But the man was just so cute. Trying to sneak in and leave pie on her desk. She'd seen him Tuesday and again yesterday and been expecting him today. Yes, he was goofy, but he was fun and kind and—did she mention?— cute.

Was it any wonder she'd checked her watch every ten minutes for the past hour? She pulled her compact and lipstick from her purse and fixed her makeup again, smoothing her hair.

She still didn't like the red color. It was one thing for a woman to dye her hair if she was happy with the results— like Mrs. Percer, the woman who'd watched Cara when she was little. But, though the shade Cara had used looked right with her eyes and skin tone, it still felt like a disguise.

The phone rang.

"Mayor Findley's office," she said, sliding her makeup back in her purse. "This is Cara."

"Cara? It's Will. I'm sorry, but I have to cancel."

"Cancel?"

"We've got a big story we're working on," he said. "We'll be late going to press, and I know your lunch time is set."

"I see." Cara frowned at the container of pie. She was all too familiar with big stories in the media.

"There was a fire on a cul-de-sac on the west side of town. Three homes destroyed, and three more damaged. A house near the middle had stored gasoline that exploded."

"Exploded? Wow."

"It's a miracle no one was hurt. Anyway, we ripped up the front page. This is important."

"I...I understand," she said, trying to sound as if she did. "I guess something like that is big news. You need to report it." But she didn't like it. It might not be a story of scandal, might not ruin anyone's life. Even so, those people were having a hard enough time already. Did they really need their misery plastered all over the front page for everyone to gawk at?

"Yeah, it is big," Will said. "But within an hour, everyone in town will know about the fire. It's more about getting the story out because there are eight kids plus their parents who lost everything. We're running a list of clothing sizes and places where people can drop off donations."

"Oh-hh." She hadn't even thought of that. "I can run out tonight and buy some things for the kids."

"What?" Will's voice was muffled. "They need me in the back shop," he said more clearly. "I'll call you later."

Cara hung up, then looked back at the container of pie on her desk.

She'd thought that over lunch she'd get to know Will better.

But maybe, even though lunch was canceled, she'd gotten to know something important about him.

Because she'd learned that in his work as a journalist, Will Hamlin wasn't trying to make money by reporting on someone else's misery. He was trying to do good, helping his fellow citizens.

Just the qualities Cara wanted in a man.

It was already twenty minutes past noon, twenty minutes past the time Will should have approved the last page so the printing plates could be made.

He walked into the newsroom from the back shop and stood, shifting his weight from one foot to the other, as he waited on one last story, a sidebar list that they'd run in a box.

Kirk's fingers flew, typing up the clothing sizes and basic needs that Cyndi was relaying over the phone.

Velma paced near the doorway to the back shop, reading backward through the typeset copy of the main fire story, checking for typos.

Russell, who had written the main story, leaned over the paste-up tables in the back shop, his blond hair sticking up on one side as if he'd run his fingers through it. He held a peanut butter sandwich in one hand, a blue pen in the other, and was marking places to cut another story below the fold. The layout system wasn't perfect. Articles were often a few lines too long and had to be adjusted with an X-Acto knife to fit the space on the page.

Except for page one, the rest of the paper was ready to go, the plates already made.

Will checked his watch. Twenty-three minutes past twelve.

Every minute meant a delay in when the presses would roll, when the delivery trucks would leave the building, when the papers would reach the public. And time, as Dad had reminded him, was money.

But this, this was why he'd gone into journalism. The adrenaline that hit the newsroom as the staff tried to achieve both accuracy and speed. The service to the community. The team effort on news that really mattered.

And this fire coverage, well... Will didn't spend much time thinking about his material possessions. But what if in a few hours his big TV, that comfy recliner he got on sale, and his baseball card collection were all gone? Even worse, what would it be like to tell a son that *his* baseball card collection was gone?

He took way, way too much for granted.

The least he could do was help those three families the best way he knew how—by rallying the whole town to support them.

"I'm finished," Kirk yelled, ripping the page out of his typewriter.

At twelve forty-seven, Will checked the new front page one last time and handed it to the pressman.

Finally, done.

He went back into his office and sank into his chair. He'd missed his lunch with Cara, and he was so hungry he thought he still smelled Russell's peanut butter sandwich.

Before he could eat, though, he had to make a phone

call. He reached toward the receiver.

Just then Cara—still wearing that green sweater—knocked on the open door of his office.

Talk about a welcome surprise.

"I need to get back," she said. "But I wanted to drop this off." She placed a large takeout box and a tall cup on his desk.

"What, um..." He sounded like an idiot. That sweater fritzed out his brain.

Then the aroma of onion rings hit his nose, and his mouth watered. He popped open the lid of the box. Yes! Onion rings and a cheeseburger.

Uncertainty colored her words. "It's what you like, isn't it? Janelle Cassidy suggested it."

Cara must not have been able to hear his stomach rumbling. "It's what I love," he said, snagging an onion ring and taking a bite. "But you didn't have to buy me lunch."

"Actually," Cara said. "Her husband, Carl, wouldn't let me pay. I was going to, but when I explained why I was bringing you lunch, he told me that one of the houses that burned belonged to the parents of a high school girl who's a waitress there."

"Grace Watson," Will said.

"Yeah. She dates the Cassidys' son. So they insisted on giving me your lunch for free."

"But you brought it over." And thought of him, taking time out of her own day. Almost part of the newspaper team without even knowing it. No wonder he liked her.

"I wanted to help."

"Thanks." He gobbled down another onion ring.

"Hey, tomorrow night would you like to go to a picnic?" The words blurted out before he thought them through. "At my folks' house. I mean, I understand if you're busy, but Dad's great with the grill and Mom's probably invited forty people. They'll have plenty for one more."

"Forty people?"

"I've got a big family, plus Mom always invites the neighbors and other friends and whoever she runs into at the grocery." And every one of those people would be very interested to see who he brought to a family event.

For some weird reason, he didn't care.

Cara looked off to one side, and she rubbed the back of her neck.

She was going to say no. He could feel it. He'd been too pushy. "Homegrown corn on the cob," he added.

She turned to him, chin raised. "I'd love to come to a picnic," she said. "And good job helping those families." She smiled at him, admiration shining in her eyes.

Will's chest swelled, and a warm tendril wrapped around his heart. "Thanks."

"Got to run."

Then she was gone.

But the warmth around his heart remained.

Chapter Six

"Are you sure it's all right that I didn't bring a dish?" Cara climbed out of Will's truck and glanced at his parents' white farmhouse.

"Yep." Will shut the passenger door. "Mom said since you were new to town, all we should bring was something to sit on." He reached into a grocery sack in the truck bed and pulled out a blanket.

"That's very nice of her." Cara gave the skirt of her aqua sundress a little shake to get it to fall properly. If only she could shake the idea that this evening was a mistake.

An evening with Will, who looked so handsome tonight in his tan shorts and navy Izod shirt? Not a mistake. It was everyone else who worried her.

When he'd invited her, attending his parents' picnic had seemed like a good idea, the perfect opportunity to meet people and make friends, exactly what she should be doing if she wanted to be happy here in Abundance.

But the nagging thought that she'd been pushing to the back of her mind, the realization that she'd be meeting his family on what was essentially their first date, bubbled up, more insistent and more worrisome than before. Meeting someone's parents on a first date was a terrible idea, especially since she'd never been the vivacious, sweetheart-of-the-ball, kind of girl. Never the one who bloomed in a crowd. And that was before what happened with her dad.

What if she acted so awkward that Will, his family, and his friends, all thought she was weird?

Could she ask him to take her home now so she could avoid disaster? No, that would look even weirder. She was going to have to shake off her worries and act normal.

Normal people didn't walk into a picnic staring down as though they were headed to their own execution. They made conversation, didn't they? She looked around, desperate for a topic.

"Did—did you grow up here?" Cara tipped her head toward the house.

Will pointed. "See that room, second floor on the right? That was mine. Now it's Mom's quilting room."

The house was white clapboard and two full stories, plus a third floor that might be usable space or maybe an attic. Two chimneys, a busy roofline, and lots of ornamentation. Victorian perhaps? Definitely old.

"What a fun place to be a kid." Cara let out a slow breath, releasing some of the tension from her shoulders. See? She was doing fine.

"It was. I mean, sometimes my brothers were a pain, but most of the time, it was great. I felt as if we were a team, you know?"

"That's a wonderful feeling to have." She'd had it once, from her work family at Smith Investment. And she'd loved it. In a way, that might be part of what she was seeking in a small town.

"Looking back, I can see how much Mom and Dad encouraged teamwork." Will gave a nod as if he approved of how he'd been raised. "I remember one time my brother John—he's the middle brother—got in trouble and had to weed the whole garden. We'd just been on vacation, and the weeds were bad. And it was hot, about this time of year."

Cara nodded. It didn't matter whether it was Kansas or Missouri, summer was sweltering.

"At first T.J. and I thought it was funny. We made a pitcher of lemonade and sat out there watching John work. After about half an hour, though, we felt guilty, and we helped him. It took the whole day, but Dad said it was the best the garden had looked all summer." Pride rang in Will's words.

"That was really nice of you," Cara said.

"Mom was so proud. 'Hamlins stick together,' she kept saying. She made us a pumpkin pie, my favorite, even though it was summer." Will looked off to one side with a smile. "I got to spray the whipped topping. I used almost the whole can, and then the three of us ate the pie right out of the pan." He glanced down. "Sounds silly, doesn't it?"

"No, it sounds perfect," Cara said. To be honest, Will's family sounded like the family she'd always dreamed of. Even prayed for. Not that it had done any good. "I didn't have any siblings, and my mother died when I was a baby. I don't even remember her."

Will stopped walking, rested a hand on her shoulder, and looked at her, his gaze steady. "I'm sorry," he said in a low voice.

"It's okay." She tried to sound upbeat. She was not letting her nervousness—or her bitterness—spoil this evening. She was moving forward here in Abundance, focusing on the positives, like how lovely and restful it was here on the Hamlin farm.

"How pretty," she said, pointing to a cluster of cornflowers and Queen Anne's lace.

"You and Mom think so." Will chuckled. "Dad always wants to mow that corner to get rid of the weeds."

"They aren't weeds. They're wildflowers. And they're beautiful."

Will shook his head slowly, as if his mom had made the same argument.

The smell of cooked beef filled the air as she and Will walked past a handful of kids playing Frisbee, rounded the corner of the house, and found dozens of people standing in small clusters, talking loudly. Lots of people. Too many for Will's parents to focus on one guest, like her. Perfect.

"Will, over here!" A woman waved from beside a long table. She wore a striped skirt and a hot pink T-shirt, her gray hair cut in a Dorothy Hamill style.

"Let me introduce you to Mom," he said.

Cara tugged on the bodice of her sundress, where the straps connected, to pull it up slightly. Really, did the first person she met have to be Will's mom?

The woman walked closer and reached for Cara's hands. "You must be Cara. Welcome to Abundance."

"Nice to meet you, Mrs. Hamlin." Okay, her voice was

a little shaky, but hopefully no one noticed. She simply needed to act normal. Not like she was afraid she'd make such a fool of herself that she'd never have friends in this town.

"Please, call me Mary." Will's mom squeezed Cara's hands, and her brown eyes shone, full of genuine warmth.

Warmth that melted the edges of Cara's nervousness.

"We're so glad you could join us tonight," Mary said.

Sincerity rang in her words, and Will caught Cara's gaze with his own, his eyes shining with encouragement.

Bit by bit, the last of the tension eased from Cara's shoulders. These people were truly, genuinely nice and coming to this picnic was, in spite of her paranoia, a good idea. It was the ideal way to make friends here in Abundance.

Mary gave Will a hug. "Now, you introduce her to everyone," she told him. "And—"

"Make her feel welcome," Will said in unison with his mom, his voice taking on a sing-song quality.

Mary dipped her chin and raised her eyebrows at Will—a silent scolding that was softened by the way the corners of her mouth curved up. "Teaching manners to three boys was a challenge, let me tell you. They seem to think I may have repeated myself a time or two." She laughed. "I need to check how they're doing with the corn. We'll talk later." She patted Cara's shoulder and slipped away.

Cara exhaled. Everything was going to be fine.

And apparently, Mary's teaching about manners had sunk in. Will introduced Cara again and again, starting with his family. She tried to keep everyone straight. His brother T.J. and his wife, Patsy, were both tall, and Patsy's shoulder-length hair feathered back, Farrah-Fawcett style. Their son, Earl Ray, was a toddler.

John, the brother Will had helped all those years ago with the weeding, was blonder than his brothers. His wife, Deborah, had short, permed hair, and they had a baby boy named Jack.

Will's dad, Thomas, wore glasses and had the tan, weathered skin of a man who spent his days outside. He seemed likable but quiet.

Then Will introduced the minister from his church, the family from the farm down the road, and the advertising manager at the newspaper and her husband. The faces began to blur. "You do realize," Cara whispered to Will, "that if I remember your family, I'll be doing well?"

"It's probably time for food then," he said.

As if on cue, Thomas rapped on a large, round smoker and walked to the head of the table of food. "If you'll join me in prayer," he said.

The crowd quieted, and heads bowed.

"Lord," Thomas said, "we thank you for this meal. We thank you for every person here today and the friendship they bring to our lives, and we thank you for loving us. Please watch over us. In your blessed son's name, we pray."

"Amen," the crowd said.

Cara opened her eyes and peeked over at Will while his head was still bowed. His "amen" hadn't been a routine, eager-to-get-to-dinner response. He—and many of the people around him—had sounded sincerely grateful, as if they honestly believed God cared. Not what she'd expected in this modern day and age.

Will opened his eyes. "Ready to eat?"

Cara moved toward the line, and Will handed her a plate.

"That smells incredible," Cara said, pointing to a platter of beef.

"Dad's smoked brisket."

"Did he cook it?"

"And he raised it. He's got two hundred and fifty head of Black Angus."

"Oh," Cara said. Probably some of them were the cattle she'd seen in the field across the road from the house.

Before long her plate was piled high, and Will spread the blanket he'd brought near where his brothers were eating.

Cara sat, shifted away from what felt like a rock under the blanket, and said hello to the members of Will's family around her—T.J., Patsy, John, Deborah, and—what were the little one's names?—Jack and Earl Ray.

T.J. sat next to Will, feeding little Earl Ray bites of watermelon. Juice dripped from the boy's grin.

A moment later, when his father was talking about the outlook for the high school football team, the toddler picked up a small piece of watermelon. The cube spurted from his fingers, flying a few inches up in the air.

On the other side of Earl Ray, Jack squealed.

Earl Ray grabbed another piece of watermelon and held it toward the baby.

Jack took it and squeezed, sending a stream of pink juice onto his leg.

Both boys erupted in giggles.

Deborah dabbed at the baby's leg with a napkin, then hauled him onto her lap. "You, Jack Hamlin, are far too easily led into trouble by your cousin."

"I'm not surprised." Her husband, John, wagged a finger at his brother. "Earl Ray probably takes after his dad. T.J. always was the troublemaker."

"Exactly," Will said.

The three brothers laughed. Their sound was deeper, but the carefree quality echoed the little boys' giggles.

"From what I remember, going to school with these three"—Deborah pointed to each of the Hamlin brothers in turn—"there wasn't a well-behaved one in the lot. I don't know how Mary survived."

"And yet," John said with a grin. "We all grew up to be law-abiding citizens of Abundance, and everyone loves us."

"It's true," Deborah said in a tone of feigned disgust. "But it does give me hope that I can civilize this little guy." She hugged Jack close.

Cara looked from one member of the family to another. Such great people. The warm bond between the Hamlins was unmistakable, and, for now at least, she was wrapped inside their happy circle. Did they realize how lucky they were to have a loving family and the respect of the community?

A moment later, Mr. Hamlin came over and tapped Will's shoulder. "Can you help me haul up more ice from the basement freezer?"

"Sure." Will picked up his plate and turned to Cara. "I'll be right back. Then we can get dessert." He stood and walked toward the house with his dad, polishing off a deviled egg he seemed to have intentionally saved for last. His plate had been piled high. How had he eaten it all so fast?

Cara glanced down at her own plate. Nearly empty. It was so good she'd practically gobbled it down. She picked up the last thing on her plate, part of a brisket sandwich, and took a bite.

"This is just the opportunity we need," Patsy said. Her voice rang with excitement. "So we can interroga—"

"Get to know you better," Deborah cut in. She shot Patsy a look.

Cara swallowed her bite of brisket, which suddenly seemed dry. "Uh, I'm looking forward to getting to know you too," she said slowly.

"Don't mind Patsy," Deborah said. "It's just that Will never brings anyone to family events, so having you here is a pretty big deal."

Cara set her plate down. Will never brought a date to family events? That *was* interesting.

"Now I already heard through the grapevine that you live at Fairview and you work for Imogene and your car leaked," Patsy said. "We want to hear everything else. Where you're from, what brought you to Abundance..."

Cara's heart rate kicked up, and beads of perspiration slid down her spine. She shifted on the blanket, unable to keep herself from backing away. Her paranoia had been fully justified. Coming here was a mistake.

"Yes, we want to know your shoe size, whether you really believe disco is dead..." Deborah's tone was lighter than Patsy's, but both women scooted closer as if eager for answers.

Cara rubbed her palms on the sides of her dress. What could she say? She wanted to become friends with Will's family, not lie to them. She shoved the last of the sandwich in her mouth. She couldn't answer if her mouth was full.

Her mind racing, she chewed. "I wear a size eight shoe," she said at last. "But I don't know about disco. I'm mostly a Billy Joel fan myself and uh…"

"What made you move to Abundance?" Patsy's eyes narrowed. "Not many people under thirty move here voluntarily."

Cara swallowed. How could she get out of this in one piece?

Some distance off, she spotted Will navigating the lawn chairs and blankets on his way back. Relief poured through her.

"Hi, Will," she called, scrambling to her feet. "You wanted to get dessert, didn't you? Those cakes and pies sure looked delicious."

She bent down to get her empty plate and cup, then snuck a peek at Deborah and Patsy.

They looked slightly stunned, the way people did when someone talked way too fast and came across as awkward. And rude. And suspicious.

She gave a jerky wave and a tight, I'm-not-insane smile, then quickly walked toward Will, her stomach sinking.

Oh, she knew this picnic was a mistake.

"This cake is so yummy. Thanks for pointing it out." Cara sat beside Will on the top step of the farmhouse front porch, cutting a second bite from the slice on her plate.

"Deborah's chocolate cake is always good," he said. "I think she even got a ribbon for it at the county fair." He pushed a blob of frosting back and forth on his plate. As far as he was concerned, the cake might as well have been store-bought.

Because although Dad did have two large bags of ice to bring up from the basement freezer, mostly he wanted to tell Will about the phone calls he'd gotten this afternoon. The first, from the president of a media conglomerate, was a response to feelers Dad had put out about selling the paper. Finding a buyer and a good offer wouldn't be a problem. The second call concerned their cattle. Dad hadn't even had the heart to tell Mom yet. There was a chance that an animal in the herd had brucellosis. Worst case scenario? The whole herd would need to be put down.

Will didn't need the rest spelled out. Despite the fact that *The Abundance News* had been in the family for decades, neither Mom nor Dad really cared about journalism. The farm, on the other hand, meant the world to Dad. And Mom, though raised in town, loved the farm more than anybody.

"I'm never closer to God than when I sit on my porch, drinking my coffee and watching the sunrise over the field across the road," she often said.

If the *News* continued to lose money and if Dad lost most or all of the herd, he wouldn't be able to make his loan payments. No matter how good he was with numbers, farming was a hard way to make a living. And if Mom and Dad had to choose between the farm and the paper, the paper would lose.

Cara nudged his elbow. "Are you all right?"

"I'm fine."

"You don't sound fine."

"Financial problems at the paper."

Cara gave a measured nod. "Do you want to talk about it?"

"Not really."

She sat silent for a few seconds. "You know," she said at last, "I've been reading your paper, and I like it, especially the stories about the fire that focused on how people could help and that article about the woman who visits old people to clean their glasses."

"Alice Butler."

"Yeah. The news can be so depressing, but that story made me happy I moved here."

Will's chest expanded. *See, Dad? I am doing something right.* "Thanks, Cara." He reached out and took her hand. "I try to work for two things at the paper. My first priority is helping the community."

"I can see why you want to. Abundance is a special town." Cara gazed across the fields to where the tops of the downtown buildings were just visible in the distance. "I like it here."

"Me too." Like a Fourth of July sparkler, hometown pride sputtered inside him. "But not everybody does. I dated a woman who hated Abundance. When she found out I was going to be editor and realized that I meant what I'd said all along, that I wanted to stay here, she ended things. She left town a month later."

Cara gave his hand a squeeze. "I know what that's like. The last guy I dated broke up with me and moved away too. Right when I was going through a terrible time."

Heat churned in Will's chest. What a jerk. How could a guy do that to a woman like Cara?

"Talk about a fair-weather friend." Her lips thinned, and she looked away. "So," she said, sounding falsely bright as she turned back to him. "What's the other thing you work for at the paper?"

"Truth." He glanced over at her.

She might think she was hiding it, but her features remained rigid as if her mind was still on her former boyfriend—a loser she needed to forget. Maybe talking about the paper would help.

"I want the paper to fight corruption, of course," Will said. "But I'm a stickler for verification. I never, ever want to destroy an innocent person's life with a story that's basically a lie because we haven't made sure it's accurate."

Cara tilted her head. "No," she said in an odd tone. "You wouldn't want to do that. Lies can cause so much pain." Her voice trembled with emotion.

Either she cared more about journalism than most people, or she hated lies as much as he did.

Something else to like about this woman.

She turned toward the road, and after a bit, her face relaxed.

Minutes passed, and he continued to stare at her. *Stop it, you idiot. You're making a fool of yourself.* Just because she was gorgeous and liked Abundance was no guarantee things would turn out better with her than with any of the other women he'd dated. No reason to assume there was anything magical about this relationship. With a shake of his shoulders, he turned toward the road.

More than half the cars along the driveway had left. The picnic was winding down with only a few bits of conversation and laughter floating over the drone of insects. The kids who had been playing Frisbee before were nowhere to be seen. Even the field across the road was empty, the cattle probably settled in their favorite spot down near the pond. Fireflies twinkled over the lawn, and the sweet fragrance of the old honeysuckle bush at the side of the house filled the evening air.

Bit by bit, the peace of the evening, the warmth of Cara's hand, and the steady presence of her shoulder against his soaked into Will. She didn't fidget. She didn't fill the air with needless talk. She simply sat as if she was happy just being here.

And that made him happy.

Being with her, his worries about the paper and the farm seemed to melt away. For all he knew, Dad's fears about brucellosis might be unfounded. The herd might be healthy. And the newspaper's profits weren't solely his responsibility. Advertising was what really brought in the dollars, and Veronica, the ad manager, was responsible for all that. With back-to-school coming up, the advertising department should be selling more ad space. All in all, his life was pretty good. Especially now.

"Hey," he said quietly.

"Yeah?" Cara turned to him. One of the skinny straps of her dress slipped off her shoulder, and she tugged it back into place.

Her skin looked so soft. He forced his eyes to meet hers. "I'm glad you're here tonight."

"Me too." Her blue-green eyes shone.

She was so kind. So easy to be around. And so beautiful.

He brushed his fingers through her hair, tucking one strand behind her ear.

She shifted her body on the wooden step, angling more to face him.

His pulse picked up, and he ran his fingertips down her jawline to her chin.

She drew in a breath.

He hesitated, then trailed one finger up to trace the edge of her lips. One kiss. He wanted just one kiss.

Her chest rose and fell, inches from his.

Slowly he slid his fingers away from her lips, skimming them over the smooth skin of her shoulders as he drew her against him.

Her pupils widened, and he felt as if he was sinking into them.

With his pulse pounding, he lowered his mouth to meet hers.

Her lips parted, and she wrapped her arms around him, pulling him closer,

Heat rushed through him and—

The porch light burst on above them, and the screen door banged open.

He jerked back.

"There you are, Will," Patsy said, sounding oblivious to what she'd interrupted. "Your mom is fixing plates to take home. She wants to know if you want some brisket."

Will spun to face his sister-in-law. "Um, no thanks, Patsy."

He looked back at Cara.

Her cheeks were pink, and her eyes swirled with embarrassment and excitement.

Way to have the worst timing ever, Patsy. Brisket was the last thing on his mind. He wanted to keep kissing Cara.

Because being with her felt different.

Special.

Right.

Like for years he'd been looking for her—not just any woman, but her specifically—and never known it.

And now he'd found her.

Chapter Seven

Half an hour later, Will walked Cara to the front step outside her apartment.

Night had nearly fallen, and she'd forgotten to leave her porch light on. Her neighbors' lights on either side were out as well. Apparently, they were away for the weekend or had gone to bed early. Only a faint glow shone from her kitchen window, and it gave about as much light as a single firefly. Unlocking her door in the near darkness might be tricky.

On the other hand, she rather liked the idea of saying goodnight to Will without a spotlight. Especially if he happened to kiss her again. Which she sincerely hoped he would.

"It's been a lovely evening," she said. She adjusted her grip on the paper plate that held a slice of Deborah's cake. Mary had insisted she bring it home for later. "Thanks for inviting me to the picnic."

"I'm glad you came. I really enjoyed spending time with you." He stepped closer.

A flutter of anticipation raced through her. He was going to kiss her again. "I really enjoyed it too."

"Can I—" he took the plate and set it on the step—"ask you out again sometime?" He caught her fingers in his, caressing them gently.

The warmth of his hands seemed to flow through her whole body. "You can," she said softly. "You don't even need to sneak into my office and leave me pie."

He laughed. "That's good." His voice deepened. "Because I plan to ask you out a lot."

He slipped his hands around her waist.

Her breath caught, and she melted against him, running her hands up his arms until they rested on his shoulders.

In the dim light, every sensation seemed intensified— the faint breeze ruffling her hair, the feel of his muscles under his shirt, and the warmth of his chest against hers.

Then he leaned down, his face hidden in shadows, and kissed her.

Her heart pounded.

The kiss on the farmhouse porch had been wonderful, full of that fluttery, heady sensation of knowing that he felt the attraction between them too.

This kiss was different.

The darkness. The privacy. The connection she felt as he pulled her tighter against him.

This kiss was no longer tentative.

For a few moments, all she knew, all she wanted to know, was the feel of his hands on her shoulders and his lips on hers. Nothing mattered but Will.

At last, he stepped back and dropped his hands to his sides.

The evening air, which had to be at least eighty degrees, felt cool on her shoulders compared with the warmth of his hands.

"Goodnight, Cara." His voice sounded huskier than before.

"Goodnight, Will," she whispered. But she didn't move. She stood there, dazed.

In the back of her mind, some semblance of thought wafted up. She needed to unlock the door and go inside. Not grab the man and kiss him again.

And again.

With a jerk, she pulled her shoulder bag in front of her and blindly pawed through it for her keys. After a bit of fumbling, she unlocked the door and opened it.

Light now shone out from her kitchen, and she took the cake plate that he held toward her.

Then she gazed at him, at the stunned tenderness in his eyes she hadn't been able to see in the darkness.

It hadn't just been her. This kiss had been different for him as well.

She drew in a deep breath, went in her apartment, and closed the door.

Inside, Cara sank onto her couch, waiting for her heart rate and breathing to return to normal. At last she stood, carried one of her kitchen chairs to the little patio off her living room, and sat down.

The wooded area at the back of the yard was entirely dark except for the stars twinkling above her, and the apartment complex was unusually peaceful, without even the sound of a neighbor's TV.

Slowly, her brain cells seemed to re-engage, still tingly from Will's kiss, but at least functioning again.

And those brain cells said that if she couldn't have more of Will's kisses, she should have cake. She let out a loud sigh, then stepped back inside. She returned with Deborah's dessert, a fork, and a glass of milk, which she sat on the milk crate patio table the previous tenant had left behind.

Cara took a bite. Man, this was good cake. Incredible frosting.

But not as incredible as the connection she'd sensed with Will. She'd felt so special, as if he truly cared, as if something more could develop. And those kisses...

Those kisses.

But what about the fact that he was a journalist? Going to a picnic with him was one thing, but should she really be kissing him? Making herself vulnerable? Because journalists had caused her so much pain. So very much pain.

She'd give anything to erase those terrible memories from her mind. Such a horrible, horrible time. Her father's company had been investigated and shut down by the FBI. His home and most of his assets seized, to one day be liquidated to reimburse the victims. And Cara, who'd worked in the accounting department of the firm, had been grilled over and over about his Ponzi scheme.

She should have figured it out. But she had been

ignorant, completely ignorant. She'd never thought of her father that way. Even when things had seemed off a time or two, she'd explained it away in her mind, giving him the benefit of the doubt.

Eventually, though, that ignorance had saved her. She was no longer a suspect.

But when he was convicted, when she finally got home from that horrible day in court, she had cried until her eyes were raw and her face and neck broke out in bright red blotches. Until all she could do was rock on the floor of her bedroom, curled up in a tight ball, as if that might somehow stop the burning ache inside her.

Just remembering it made her chest hurt again.

She'd been so alone. So incredibly alone.

Both her parents had been only children, both raised by elderly parents. All her grandparents were gone before she turned ten. For years it had just been Cara and her father and—until she moved when Cara was twelve—Mrs. Percer, her babysitter.

As a child, Cara had prayed for a mom, prayed for more family. But God had ignored her. Then He took the only family she had, her work family and her father. Oh, her father hadn't been perfect, but growing up she'd at least believed he loved her.

After his arrest, though, he'd sent word that he didn't want to see her.

And then, when it seemed things couldn't get any worse, they did. Because of the media.

Those pushy creeps had hovered outside her apartment, hounding her every time she stepped out the door. They'd taken every horrid detail of her dad's arrest and made it uglier. They'd twisted the facts and written stories that made it sound as if she'd been involved.

Her boyfriend, who also worked at Smith Investment, had dumped her. He'd scrambled to find another job and moved away to start a new life. Without her. Her work friends—or people she'd thought were her friends—had gotten off the phone as fast as possible when she called. And people on the street had pointed at her.

At last, she'd run away, checking into a hotel outside Kansas City for a week. Perhaps, if she'd felt stronger, she might have called a friend from college. But what if she had explained what had happened, and the line had gone silent? What if instead of sympathy and compassion she got only mumbling and rejection? No, it was better if no one from college knew. So she'd sat, alone in that hotel room, eating room service and figuring out what to do next.

She'd come to two conclusions. Spottsville could no longer be home. And blond Ann Smith, daughter of Baxter Smith, could no longer exist.

She wasn't committing fraud. She still used her real name, Caroline Ann Smith, on her driver's license. And lots of women colored their hair. But not that many colored their hair on the same day they began going by a different name.

She took another bite of Deborah's cake, one with plenty of frosting.

What kind of life was she going to have here if she got involved with a reporter? Reporters were aggressive and rude and only cared about themselves. They didn't care about the people they hurt. And Will was…

Nothing like that.

She stared down at the remaining cake, a sad little bite that she'd smushed with her fork.

Then she looked at the sky, where more stars had appeared, and she pictured Will's face.

The ache in her chest eased.

Will was kind. And funny. And he'd helped her. With her laundry and her car and the people he'd introduced her to.

And his focus at the newspaper seemed to be on helping the community.

He might be a journalist, but he was different. Look at what he'd said. "I never, ever want to destroy an innocent person's life with a lie." That didn't sound like the reporters back in Spottsville.

No, Will Hamlin had good character, in his personal life and in his work life.

And he was someone she could count on. Someone who wouldn't abandon a friend—or a girlfriend—in a time of trouble. He was someone she could trust, maybe even one day trust with her past. Someone she *should* one day trust with her past if she wanted a real relationship.

And who knew? Maybe she did.

One thing she did know.

Even if she'd made a total fool of herself in front of Deborah and Patsy, she was glad she'd gone to the Hamlin's picnic.

Chapter Eight

"Sorry I'm late," Kirk said, rushing into the Tuesday afternoon staff meeting. "I just got a tip about Abundance High's prospects this fall. A new kid transferred in with a great arm."

"Excellent." Will leaned back in his chair. When the local football team was on a winning streak, newspaper sales rose. Everybody wanted to read the details of a good game. "So, I only have one thing to discuss this week. The fire coverage. You guys did a fantastic job pitching in and working as a team." He smiled at each one in turn. "Exactly the type of journalism I want our paper known for—timely, up-to-the-minute information that serves our community. Good job."

Russell and Kirk mumbled their thanks. Velma sat up straighter and smoothed her gray hair.

Cyndi beamed. "It was so exciting. I mean, I know it was awful, and I'm sorry those families lost their homes, but it was cool feeling that we were in the middle of things. That the paper really mattered."

"The paper always matters," Velma said firmly. "People don't realize how important it is to have a local newspaper, a source where they can get information they can trust."

"Velma's right," Russell said. "But I know what you mean, Cyndi. Wait until you work an election night. You'll love the newsroom then."

Will nodded. "Election nights are my favorite times to be a journalist too."

Even Velma tipped her head to one side as if acknowledging that Russell had a good point.

"I don't know," Kirk said. "You can't compare anything political with that time I got to cover the basketball team winning the district championship in the last second of overtime." He gave a satisfied sigh. "Now that was exciting." His voice warmed, and a note of humor crept in. "But maybe you have to be a sports writer. Maybe you news people don't have the savvy to appreciate it."

Everyone laughed, including Will. What a good group he had. The thought of having this camaraderie spoiled by the changes that would result if the *News* was bought by a chain... No, *The Abundance News* was a solid, respectable newspaper. With some hard work, they could make it a great paper, a paper that was such a vital part of the community that circulation and advertising would rise to where Dad would never consider selling.

"Hey," Cyndi said. "I have a story idea. A big one."

Will leaned farther back in his chair, ready for her pitch.

"My friend Sheryl's dad runs The Food Barn. He's been making her work there all summer as a cashier. Talk about a terrible idea." Cyndi waved one hand as if to dismiss the thought.

Will frowned. What was a bad idea? Her story idea? Or her friend working as a cashier? What kind of story about The Food Barn, their largest advertiser, did she think she had?

"Sheryl's... She's not that good at math." Embarrassment, then guilt crossed Cyndi's brown eyes. "I bought a candy bar in her lane once, and it took her forever to make change."

Velma cleared her throat. "The news story?"

"Well, Sheryl's parents are closing The Food Barn. They're moving to St. Louis."

A sudden coldness hit Will's core. He leaned forward so fast that his chair gave a distinct click. The Food Barn couldn't be closing. He must have heard wrong.

But Velma had gone pale, and Russell had frozen, ballpoint pen hanging from his mouth.

"Don't you think it would be a good story?" Cyndi twisted her head from side to side, glancing at the others, then she looked back at Will. "I mean, The Food Barn has way better selection than Crupes Grocery. I bet when it's gone my mom will probably go over to Prattsville or Miller's Junction to do her shopping. That seems like news."

Will swallowed, his mouth too chalky to speak.

"Cyndi, are you sure?" Russell said.

"Well, Sheryl should know. Her family already went house-hunting in Chesterfield." Cyndi looked around again. "That's a suburb on the west side of St. Louis. I have friends from college who live there."

"Dear," Velma said in a flat tone, "we know where Chesterfield is. I don't think you realize what this means."

"Yeah," Russell said. "This is serious."

Will let out a shaky breath. "Serious" didn't begin to cover what happened when a newspaper lost a big insert every Sunday, especially if that newspaper was barely getting by.

"I don't understand," Cyndi said.

"The Food Barn is the biggest advertiser in *The Abundance News*." Kirk ran a hand over his brow. "And I was about to tell you all that my wife's pregnant again."

"Oh, Kirk." Velma reached over and patted his back.

The icy feeling inside Will spread to his stomach, freezing his lunch into a jagged lump. Here he was thinking about how his life would be affected if Dad sold the paper. If he was any kind of manager he should be thinking of his staff.

No chain was going to get rid of local sports coverage. It was too vital to circulation. But if *The Abundance News* was bought by a chain that owned a nearby paper, the chain might make Kirk cover stories for both areas. Then he'd never see his family. Or—even worse—they might do the reverse and have a staff member from a nearby paper cover Abundance and let Kirk go.

And Velma was even more at risk. The wires were full of great features a chain could run.

"It's not like the *News* makes piles of money, Cyndi," Russell said. "Things are going to get bad if we lose the money from The Food Barn."

"And…" Will's voice came out in a croak. "If Crupes is the only grocery store left in town, it won't have much reason to advertise, and it's our second biggest account."

Russell stared at the floor.

Velma twisted her hands together in her lap.

And Kirk looked like he might throw up.

Exactly how Will felt.

How on earth was he going to keep Dad from selling the paper now?

If only everyone did what they were supposed to, things would work out.

Like if everyone gave the copier time to cool down between runs, the machine would perform without a hitch.

Cara hit the Start button.

The green light came on, and the first sheet slid in with a whir, just as it should. Working on this project first thing was a great idea. She'd get these copies made for Imogene while everyone else in city hall was settling in to begin their Wednesday. And since the copier had been sitting quietly all night, it wouldn't be overheated from previous jobs. It would easily handle her project.

Which was sizable. Sixty copies of a twenty-page booklet with a card stock front and back to be ready before the Chamber of Commerce meeting Friday morning. She'd have to collate and staple them tomorrow though. Today she also had fourteen letters to type and send out.

The next sheet of paper eased in from the feeder tray, and Cara propped her hip against the copy room counter.

Will hadn't called last night. She wouldn't see him for

lunch today or tomorrow either, not with all Imogene had her doing. Maybe he would call tonight. Not that she was pining away for him, planning her evenings so she'd be home if the phone rang.

Well, maybe she was a little.

But she sure wasn't going to let him know that.

The copier finished its run, and she lined up the next page on the glass and lowered the lid. Then she ran a hand over the papers in the "Done" tray. A bit warm, but not hot and not smelling as if they'd been baked. She waited a few seconds, gave the machine a good-dog pat, hit Start, and propped one hip against the counter.

Twenty minutes later, though, the copier had jammed four times.

"Piece of junk," she muttered. So much for performing without a hitch.

She'd wasted six sheets of paper because she got flustered and put her original on the glass crooked. She had a smear of ink on the sleeve of her white blouse from having to reach deep inside to pull out two sheets of stuck paper. And if she was getting those fourteen letters out today, she needed to start typing now and finish her copying after the mail went out mid-afternoon.

By that time, the copier would be in high demand. Every time she stopped to let it cool down, someone would come in, pretend they didn't notice her, slide their paper into the machine, and hit Start.

She glared at the copier one more time and began to gather up her project.

"Cara, here you are." DeeDee came in and shut the door. Her lips were drawn into a line.

"Are you all right?" Cara stepped closer and laid a hand on DeeDee's arm.

"No." DeeDee's voice was strained. "Can I tell you something in the strictest confidence?"

"Of course."

"Francine has to meet with an outside accountant today. They think there might be money missing."

The base of Cara's throat grew tight. "How much?"

"More than ten thousand dollars," DeeDee said. "I'm not even supposed to know, but I overheard when I was transferring a call."

Cara drew in a quick breath. Ten thousand dollars was a lot of money. No wonder Imogene had been on the phone so much with her door closed.

"What if everyone says I took it?" DeeDee bit her lip.

A distinct possibility, but Cara wouldn't say that. She wrapped an arm around the older woman's shoulders. "I bet a couple of numbers got transposed. The outside accountant will figure it out."

"You think so?"

"Of course." At least Cara hoped so. A foolish, misguided hope given the way the world worked, but... She gave a stiff smile.

DeeDee let out a breath, and tension eased in her shoulders. "I prayed about this, but as soon as I stopped praying, I started worrying again."

"Stop worrying. You are the absolute last person anyone in city hall would accuse of stealing." That, at least, was true.

"Thank you." DeeDee pulled her into a hug, then took a half step back. "I guess I better get to my desk. And reread that sign I put up to remind me that God answers prayers."

With effort, Cara did not roll her eyes. She didn't want to be rude, but she also didn't want DeeDee trusting in something that wasn't going to help. "Do you really believe that?"

"I certainly do. But he doesn't always answer as fast as you'd like. Or the way you want."

"That's for sure," Cara said, unable to keep the sarcasm out of her words. Because she knew all too well that sometimes he answered with silence. Or a series of events that made it clear that even if she hadn't heard it, he'd answered with a loud, resounding *no.*

"I don't mean it like that," DeeDee said. "I mean sometimes he answers in a way that's better than anything you would have thought of." She gave a firm nod as if assuring herself. "And sometimes he says no because he has something better in mind down the road."

Cara's stomach sank, and she looked down at her copies. What else could she say?

DeeDee might be in major denial, but Cara knew the truth. Even if a woman was innocent, even if she did what she was supposed to, if money went missing, her life could be ruined by speculation and innuendo.

God wasn't going to help that.

Chapter Nine

Once again, Will had hope.

On the sidewalk outside the *News*, he waved goodbye to Veronica at the twin doors of the paper. The door on the left led straight upstairs to advertising. The door on the right led to the newsroom on the first floor. Most of the time news and advertising didn't interact much. Yes, they shared the same photographer and sometimes squabbled over his time, and they worked together for special advertising supplements like the annual progress edition or the spring bridal supplement. But as the two doors symbolized, the two departments were set up to operate independently. Yesterday, though, Will had called Veronica and said they had to talk.

He'd picked up lunch for both of them and met her in Rose Park. The small park, located at the eastern edge of downtown, was the perfect place for him to tell her that The Food Barn might close—without anyone else hearing.

Ever since the staff meeting yesterday, he'd worried about the future. But at lunch today, Veronica, who he'd expected to panic, had actually seen the closing of The Food Barn as a way to bring in more advertising. At first, he'd thought she was crazy, but her plan made sense.

Life was going to work out after all. Veronica and her staff were committed to increasing the ad revenue. And on the way back from lunch, he'd had an idea to draw more readers, an idea he planned to tell his staff as soon as possible.

He lived in a wonderful town. And he was dating a great girl. He even had a surprise in mind for her later this evening.

Now he stopped under the AC vent by Kim's desk. Two o'clock on a Wednesday afternoon. His staff should be finished with lunch, out on interviews, on the phone nailing down details for tomorrow's stories, or typing up those stories. Instead, Russell and Kirk were arguing over something, Cyndi was rubbing cream on her fingernails, and Velma was reorganizing her bulletin board.

No wonder the paper was struggling. His staff wasn't even trying.

Wait. They might need some renewed hope as well.

"Hey everybody, come in my office a minute," he said. "I've got news."

Kirk looked over, his mouth tensed. "I don't think I want to hear it."

Velma glanced at him. "I guess I could retire," she said. "I mean, I don't have as much saved up as I should, but I may not have a choice."

Will waved them into his office, hurrying them along.

This attitude needed to stop. Now.

Once they were all inside, he shut the door and sat down. "I had lunch with Veronica," he said, not even waiting for Kirk and Russell to unfold their chairs. "I think we overreacted yesterday."

Kirk focused on his chair as if what Will had said didn't even register. Russell sat and stared at the floor. Not one face showed a sign of optimism.

Will continued. "She says they brought in three new accounts last week."

"I bet they'll buy those dinky little ads that run on page seven," Russell said. "Maybe one ad every six months."

Will huffed out a breath. "And she says if The Food Barn goes out of business, the grocery stores in Prattsville and Miller's Junction will see a chance to get the Abundance shoppers. They'll want to advertise in the *News*."

"Will," Velma said in a tone that rang with pity. "Don't you see what's happening? Veronica has to put on a good front for you. Your dad's the publisher. She's not going to tell you the truth, which is that it's hopeless."

"Working here is like being a waiter on the Titanic." Russell sank lower in his chair. "It's only a matter of time before we go under."

Will scanned the room. Not a single member of his staff was listening to what he was saying. They were too busy wringing their hands and giving up. Granted, the situation wasn't ideal, but this wasn't the time to abandon ship, and the *News* wasn't the Titanic.

Will looked up at his copy of *All the President's Men*. At least while Woodward and Bernstein were investigating

Nixon, they didn't have to worry about *The Washington Post* going to the highest bidder at a fire sale. But most importantly, they probably didn't work with such...

"Quitters." The word burst from his mouth. Name calling didn't seem like good leadership, but since he was already headed down this path, he kept going. "You all are acting like a bunch of quitters."

No one disputed his assessment.

Will clenched his fists together in his lap. He was the editor-in-chief. He needed to motivate these people. "Kirk," he said, "when you were behind by two touchdowns at halftime in high school, did you stay in the locker room and moan? Or did you go back out there and fight?"

Kirk blinked. "We, uh, we fought. And"—he raised his head a fraction of an inch—"a lot of times we came back and won."

"That's what we're going to do," Will said. "We're going to fight. You guys are a great team. Remember what you did with those fire stories? We're going to trust that Veronica knows what she's talking about, and we're going to focus on our jobs—good reporting, solid features, and quality sports coverage."

No response. Every one of them still looked glum.

But he had a plan to empower them. "And we're going to attract more subscribers with new front-page features, one every weekday, Monday through Friday."

Velma jerked back. "I don't see how I can write that much more. I'm pretty busy with the daily features page. I mean, I can try but..."

"No, Velma. It won't be all you. Everyone in this

room, me included, can write one extra feature a week, not too long, but something with broad appeal to help us get new subscribers. People love to see their friends and family in the paper. I'll write the first one, starting this Friday."

"I can do an extra feature a week," Kirk said. "I've been thinking we ought to do a story on the couple that moved to town and opened that new gym over on Elm Street. I bet I can have it ready Monday."

A zing of adrenaline shot through Will. Finally, at least Kirk was getting on board. "Excellent."

"A whole extra story every week?" Cyndi said.

"Think of the clips for your portfolio," Will said. "When you graduate, you're going to need to show you can write more than obits."

"He's right about that," Russell muttered.

Will stood, hands flat on the desk. "Are you all willing to fight for the paper? To keep it in business? To make it not just the local rag, but a key part of our community?"

Silence.

Will leaned forward. "Well, are you?"

Kirk rose to his feet. "I'm willing."

Velma stood up. "Me too. I'll write something for Tuesday. I'm not ready to retire."

Cyndi twisted the hem of her skirt with one hand and looked at Russell's drooping head, then at Kirk and Velma. "I'm only here for a few more weeks, and I don't know what I should write about but..."

"I'll help you," Velma said. "I've got a file of ideas. We'll find something easy for you to do for Wednesday."

Cyndi got up as well. "I'll do my best."

Will's heart picked up speed. He could do this. He

could be a leader. He could inspire them as a real editor-in-chief should. "Russell, are you with us?" Surely his old buddy wasn't going to be the weak link.

Russell stared at the floor.

Kirk bumped his elbow against Russell's shoulder. Velma peered at him. Even Cyndi twisted up her mouth at him as if she expected better.

At last Russell raised his head. "Yeah, sure. I guess I get next Thursday." He slowly got to his feet.

"Okay." Will stretched out a fist toward the center of the room, the way his basketball coach used to do back in high school. One by one the others laid a hand atop his. Kirk, Velma, Cyndi, and—at last—Russell.

Energy surged through Will. His staff was, even if a little reluctantly, a team. They could save the paper.

Scratch that.

They *would* save the paper.

As Cara walked toward her apartment after work Wednesday, two girls, about eight and ten, roller-skated toward her on the sidewalk. The late afternoon sun bounced off the concrete like heat coming out of an oven, but the girls didn't seem to care. Their smiles were broad and their giggles lighthearted.

Cara, on the other hand, felt uneasy.

She wasn't involved in the finances of the city of Abundance. There was no reason an investigation should affect her at all. But talking with DeeDee about missing money this morning had kept her stomach in knots all day.

She shouldn't take her glum mood out on the

neighborhood though. "Hi, girls," she called.

They waved, and the older one showed off a quick spin.

Cara mustered the brightest smile she could and let herself in her apartment.

Her extremely avocado apartment.

What had she been thinking when she rented this place? She didn't care how popular the color was—avocado was ugly.

And the heat! Today had been awful. How close could the humidity get to one hundred percent before it actually rained? Plus, she'd talked to Will on Sunday and Monday, but she hadn't seen him or heard from him yesterday or today. What did that mean? Was he avoiding her? Did he regret getting closer to her?

She was trying to keep up a good attitude about starting over here in Abundance, but doubts seemed to pinch at her when she was tired or lonely. And—

What was that on her back porch?

Cara dumped her purse on the couch and walked toward the sliding glass door.

There, on the milk crate, was a glass vase of flowers.

The knots eased in her stomach.

The flowers were so sweet and beautiful, exactly what she needed to drive her doubts away.

She brought the vase inside and took the flowers out, laying them on the kitchen counter. The blossoms hadn't been arranged with the symmetry of a florist bouquet. They'd been haphazardly placed and were a bit too tall for the vase. But the huge mass of cornflowers and Queen Anne's lace was four times what she'd seen in Will's parents' yard. It looked like he had wandered outside for hours, cutting them for her.

She trimmed the stems and arranged the blossoms back in the vase, running her fingers over the cornflower petals and the delicate leaves of the Queen Anne's lace.

She added a bit more water, dried the vase, and placed it on her tiny breakfast bar.

What a thoughtful thing for him to do.

Cara sank onto a barstool and stared at the flowers. She hadn't known him that long. Just a few weeks.

But it felt longer. She was so happy when she was with him. Not only was he handsome, but he was also kind and smart, and…he made her feel like the most special girl in the world.

She hesitated, then ran one finger down the side of the vase as the realization flowed through her.

She might be a little bit in love with Will Hamlin.

Chapter Ten

The aroma of Will's special spaghetti sauce hung in the office air Thursday afternoon, hovering in a garlicky cloud around the empty Tupperware on his desk.

He pulled a napkin from the stack in his drawer and wiped a spot of sauce off his khaki pants. He'd been so focused on how to structure his Friday feature about a local beekeeper that he'd dripped part of his lunch.

He wadded the napkin, shot for the trashcan, and scored. He pumped a fist in the air. Kirk wasn't the only staff member with athletic prowess.

Will turned to his typewriter and ran his fingers across the keyboard, lingering over the letter *N*. Hal had worn almost the whole letter off his keyboard with all his typing. Day after day, article after article, the news business took consistent work. Sometimes a journalist had to give a little more, work a few more hours, write an extra feature to succeed.

Today Will was setting a good example by writing the first front-page feature. And tonight he'd call Cara to see if she'd like to go out this weekend. He could celebrate the new features running, the beginning of the staff working together to save *The Abundance News*.

From out in the newsroom, he even heard Velma and Cyndi discussing what feature Cyndi might write. Good old Velma, getting Cyndi started right away. Yep, with everyone pitching in, things would turn out fine.

He began to type.

An hour and a half later, the story about the beekeeper was nearly done. He needed to take out that awful pun he'd made in the first paragraph, asking readers if they'd heard the latest buzz. Otherwise the story wasn't half bad.

"Hey, Will?" Russell stood in the doorway. "Got a minute?"

"A couple. What's up?"

"I, uh…" Russell walked in and shut the door behind him, then perched on one of the two chairs across from Will's desk. His blond hair stuck up on top, the way it did when he ran his hands through it.

That meant Russell was stressed. Will turned to face him more directly.

Russell studied the floor and slid his hands back and forth on his pant legs. His shoulders raised and lowered, and he looked up. "I accepted a job at a paper in Florida. Circulation of almost a hundred thousand. I'll be writing local news, and they want to train me to do investigative stuff."

"Florida?" Russell was leaving? Now? What happened to pulling together as a team?

"I hate to do this to you, but things around here are kind of uncertain. Plus, you and I have butted heads a lot since you got promoted. And after yesterday, well, you know I hate writing features."

Russell wasn't only leaving for opportunity. He was leaving to get away from the way Will ran the paper. To get away from the extra features he'd assigned. "I see. You're leaving when...?"

"Before I move down there, they want me to attend a three-day workshop at Mizzou. They said if there was any way I could go, it would give me a head start."

"When is it?" The University of Missouri School of Journalism probably put on an outstanding workshop. Maybe it wasn't for another month. That would give Will plenty of time to advertise Russell's job—because there was no way Dad could possibly tell him to make do with only Cyndi—and get the new hire up to speed. There might even be a week of overlap so Russell could show the new person the ropes.

Russell shifted his weight in his chair. "The workshop starts Wednesday. I'm hoping I can use vacation days or sick days for the workshop and still be able to move to Florida in two weeks."

"Next Wednesday, six days from now?" Will's voice cracked, and heat poured through him. No way. No possible way. They were already short-staffed, making do with Cyndi. He was pretty sure Russell didn't have any vacation time coming. And an employee was supposed to give a minimum of two weeks' notice, two weeks they actually planned to work, to allow the paper time to regroup.

Will pressed his back teeth together and looked away.

On the top shelf of the bookcase, the cover of Woodward and Bernstein's book gleamed in the fluorescent light. Investigative reporting. For a paper with a circulation of a hundred thousand. Russell would be digging out corruption and finding the dirt on sleazy politicians and...well, everything a journalist could dream of. And he already had the job offer, an offer that almost certainly held more prestige and more money than the *News* could ever provide. He'd probably already started packing. In fact, he could leave today and never come back. So Will could either be professional or not.

"We can make it work, Russell. It sounds like a real opportunity."

Russell's eyes lit. "Thanks. It is. I'll be doing exactly what we used to talk about."

"I know," Will said. "Congratulations." He tried not to let bitterness seep into his words. Tried not to think about the fact that Russell's plan to pursue his dreams might mean the end of Will's. Losing his best—and only—news reporter might be the wave that sent him completely under as editor of the paper. As much as he liked Abundance, he might fail so badly that he had to go elsewhere and start back at the bottom as the reporter who wrote all the obits. Just when he'd believed things at the *News* were getting better. Just when he'd met a nice girl who liked his hometown. He blew out a long breath, then scanned the calendar on the wall. "So you'll be gone...?"

"Next Wednesday, Thursday, Friday." Russell ticked them off on his fingers. "I'll leave you a feature to run Thursday and come back in on Saturday, and I'll be here until September 5. And I've got a lead on a big story. One that should draw a lot of readers."

Will raised an eyebrow.

"There might be money missing from the city treasurer's office. Big money, not like that mowing story."

Will moved forward in his chair. "Really?" A solid investigative piece might boost circulation.

"What I have so far is shaky, a bunch of files I don't understand. The person who gave them to me won't even let me quote them as 'a source in city hall.' They say there shouldn't be any developments until next week. By then, I'll be back here and all over it."

Will slumped and rubbed the base of his scalp. The story had to be weak if Russell called it shaky. And Will had a hard time believing money would be missing where DeeDee worked. "Okay," he said. "You might even learn something at Mizzou that will help you nail it down." More likely, though, what he'd learn was not to believe every crackpot rumor that floated around town. Will had been down this road with Russell before.

"Thanks," Russell gave an awkward wave and left.

Will scrubbed a hand over his face. What a mess. Even getting through Russell's days at the workshop would be a challenge, not to mention when he was gone for good. The paper still had to come out every day, but Will also needed to figure out how and where to advertise Russell's position and then talk to Dad about hiring a replacement.

More than he could think about right now.

When he had his own feature to finish writing.

The moment Cara walked out the back door of city hall at the end of the day, her eyes were drawn past the parking lot, across Ninth Street, to the newspaper building.

No sign of Will.

She'd tried to call him last night to thank him for the flowers, but he hadn't been home. She'd phoned again at work today after she thought the paper would have gone to press, but he hadn't been available. And he hadn't returned her call.

But all day, which had been such a good day without a single word about missing money, she'd remembered her pretty wildflower bouquet waiting for her at home. And, after talking with DeeDee, she'd decided they had worried needlessly over what might only be a typo.

A pickup truck passed on Ninth, but it wasn't blue. It wasn't Will's. And no one came out the door of the paper. She hesitated on the sidewalk, hoping everything was all right. Perhaps it was just a busy news day.

As if in answer to her prayers, he rounded the corner of city hall, turning from Main onto Ninth. He carried a Styrofoam box that looked as if it came from Cassidy's, and his face was drawn up in concentration.

Her heart did a little double step. Not the sort of thing that happened when she saw a friend, even one she'd been hoping to see. No, that double step was confirmation of what she'd suspected last night. She was falling for him.

"Will!" She hurried across the parking lot.

He looked up, waved and gave a slight smile, then walked to meet her.

"I'm so glad to see you," she said. "Thank you for the wildflowers. They're beautiful."

"I'm glad you like them."

"Hey, how's your day been? I called earlier, but they said you couldn't come to the phone."

"You did? I didn't even see the message." Will yanked at his tie, loosening it. "Frankly, it's been a horrible day. Russell's leaving."

"The guy who writes most of the news stories besides you?"

"Yeah. Barely giving any notice. I grabbed a sandwich at the diner." Irritation rang in Will's voice. "I'm going to stay late and try to figure out how to manage until we can hire a replacement."

Oh, poor Will. He'd been worried enough about the paper before. He didn't need this too. "I'm so sorry. It's never good to be short-staffed."

"Especially when you're the one who has to pick up most of the slack." He shot an annoyed look at the newspaper office. "I don't mean to complain." His tone brightened as he turned back to face her. "It really is nice to see you."

"I think it's okay to complain when you have something like this thrown at you." She laid a hand gently on his arm. "But I bet when you sit down and focus, you'll find an answer. I have a feeling you're awfully good at what you do."

"You're kind to say that, but you may be the only person in town who thinks that way." He gave a wry smile.

"What about that nice story you wrote about the woman who cleans people's glasses? I can't be the only person who liked it."

He hesitated. "Well, no, you weren't."

"See? Things aren't all bleak." She nodded her encouragement. "The news about Russell was probably just sudden. You'll figure things out."

Will let out a sigh, and his chin rose a notch. His lips curved up, and his eyes brightened. "Thanks, Cara. Running into you was exactly what I needed."

Her chest tingled. Her little words of encouragement had helped. And the look in his eyes... Was it wishful thinking to hope he might feel the same way about her as she did about him? "Good," she said. "I'm glad."

"All right." He stood up straighter. "I better get to work." He raised the box with his dinner in salute and headed toward the newspaper.

Cara waved and turned toward her car.

A few encouraging words were good, but she could do more to cheer him up.

Starting with a quick trip to the grocery store.

Chapter Eleven

Will picked up the yellow legal pad from the desk, reread his rough ideas for getting along without Russell, and stretched his back against his chair. It had been three hours since he'd seen Cara outside city hall, but—despite frequent thoughts about the color of her eyes and the softness of her lips—he'd made some progress on a plan for the next few weeks.

He'd found a folder that Hal had left with information about how to advertise a position, and he'd worked up the wording for a job posting. With reluctance, he'd decided that the front-page features would have to be cut back to three days a week until the new reporter was hired and up to speed. He couldn't expect Kirk or Velma to write more than one extra feature a week, and he was going to need Cyndi to cover hard news. He just had to figure out where she would do the least damage.

A soft rattle echoed from the newsroom.

Will paused and listened for a second.

Nothing but silence. It must have been the air conditioning. Or maybe someone working late up in advertising.

He needed to make a list of meetings to have Cyndi cover and—

Someone rapped on the window behind him.

His heart jolted, and he jerked upright, then spun around.

There, standing right outside his window, was Cara.

He waved, held up one finger, and hurried to open the main door.

"Hey," she said as she came in. "I saw the way you jumped. I didn't mean to startle you. I knocked but…"

"I heard something, but I thought it was the air conditioner." Will laughed. Man, she looked beautiful. She'd changed out of her work clothes and was wearing a T-shirt and blue shorts that showed off her long legs.

"What brings you by?" he said, trying not to be too obvious with his perusal of her legs or the plate she was carrying.

"I made you cookies. Peanut butter butterscotch crispy treats. Try one." She peeled back the plastic wrap covering them.

Will grabbed one and took a bite. The cookies were cold like they'd been refrigerated. They were firm, almost like fudge, not chewy like regular Rice Krispies Treats. And the combination of flavors was delicious. "These are incredible." He polished off the rest of the cookie in one bite.

Cara glanced down, her eyelashes brushing her now-pink cheeks. "I wouldn't go that far," she said as she looked back up at him. "But I'm glad you like them."

Will eyed the rest of the cookies. "Is that whole plate for me?" He reached for it, then stopped. "I mean, um, I don't mean to be rude…"

"You're not being rude." She held the plate toward him. "You're the reason I made them. I noticed you didn't have a separate container for pie when you brought dinner back from Cassidy's. I wondered if cookies might make working late a little better."

Will took the plate and selected another cookie, the largest one he saw. "Definitely." Gorgeous and thoughtful. No wonder he enjoyed being around her.

"Are you figuring things out?" she asked.

"Yeah. What you said helped. You made me focus on finding solutions instead of just being upset. I am disappointed, though. I wanted to take you out this weekend. But any time I'm not putting out the paper, I'll have to spend getting ads posted for Russell's position and planning how to adjust news coverage. I can't work eighteen hours a day, six days a week until the position is filled."

"You won't have to do that, will you?"

"No, we can use more wire stories, and there are a couple of other things we can do short term."

"Then this weekend is nothing to worry about," she said. "I need to find a few things for my apartment. Once you get things under control, we can go out next week. In fact, I should let you get back to work." She walked toward the door.

He set the cookies on the counter by Kim's desk and

hurried after her. Sure, maybe she wanted to get home and get a good night's sleep before work tomorrow, but he hadn't meant to imply that she should leave.

Outside, he caught up with her beside her car. "Hey, thank you. The cookies are great, and it means a lot that you came by." He reached out to grab her hand in his.

"I wanted you to know I'd been thinking of you," she said.

"And you're sure you're not feeling as though I'm blowing you off this weekend?"

"No," she said in a calm, easy tone. "I understand work crises happen. Just hang in there." She gave his hand a quick squeeze and climbed in her car.

He stepped back and waved as she drove away. After her visit, his whole body felt lighter.

She'd been thinking of him.

She'd brought him cookies.

And she was understanding about the mess at work. Not making him feel guilty as he knew his old girlfriend would have been. Instead, she'd been encouraging.

Cookies, understanding, those gorgeous blue-green eyes, and those long legs.

He moaned. Focusing on the issues of the newspaper was going to be a struggle.

Almost done.

At ten minutes after five the following Tuesday, when nearly everyone else in city hall had gone home, Cara positioned the heavy-duty stapler next to the last booklet and forced the top down with both hands.

The stapler emitted a firm *thwunk*, the sound it made when it worked properly. Too bad it required so much force to get it to do that. Imogene had wanted twenty more copies of the booklet for a regional development meeting tomorrow, and Cara was almost at the end. Eighteen booklets were done with two staples in each, not to mention the staples she'd had to pull out and re-do because they didn't go all the way through. No wonder the heels of both her hands were tender.

She added one more staple to the nineteenth booklet and placed it on the completed pile on her desk.

Imogene had offered to stay and help, but Cara knew that every Tuesday evening she had her exercise class at five thirty. Besides, staying an extra fifteen or twenty minutes once in a while wasn't a big deal. Not if it meant job security. Because the longer she lived in Abundance, and the more time she spent with Will Hamlin, the more she liked it here.

She had been a bit down over the weekend, wishing she could see him, but she understood, and he had called Saturday and again last night. Just talking to him on the phone had made her so happy. He was smart and funny and had a way of looking at things that showed her his kind heart. And made her really glad she'd moved to Abundance.

She lined up the last booklet and used her arm muscles to drive the staple in, then added the booklet to the pile. Twenty copies, all ready for the morning. Perfect. Imogene would be pleased.

Somewhere in the hallway, a woman's heels clicked hurriedly on the tile, echoing in the empty building. The heels clicked closer, and DeeDee appeared in the doorway, clutching a stack of papers to her chest.

"I didn't realize you were still here," Cara said.

"I shouldn't be. There's a woman in my Sunday school class who's ill, and it's my night to make dinner for her and her three kids. But I need to talk to you. Has Imogene left?"

"Right at five. Exercise class."

"That's what I thought." DeeDee came in and pulled the door closed behind her. "Cara, I have a favor to ask." Her voice shook.

"Sure. What can I do?"

"I understand if you say no, but I was hoping..." DeeDee paused, then her words spilled out. "After Francine and Rachel left, I pulled a bunch of files and copied them. I know I work in the treasurer's office, and you work for Imogene, but you have a background in accounting. Can you take a look to see if anything strikes you as odd? Maybe you're right. Maybe I transposed some numbers."

"I..." Cara straightened her pile of booklets. She wanted to help DeeDee. The older woman had been so kind and—besides Will—was her only real friend in Abundance. And, though Cara didn't like to dwell on it, DeeDee didn't have as much training in accounting as she did. She certainly didn't want DeeDee to be wrongly accused of theft.

Tension built in her chest, and she ran a hand back and forth along the edge of the booklets.

She had to calm down. It was paranoid to think that people would connect what was probably a mathematical error in Abundance with her father's crimes.

"Please," DeeDee said.

Cara stepped toward DeeDee. She was being ridiculous, letting fear keep her from being a good friend. "I'd be happy to look things over."

DeeDee handed her the papers and wrapped her arms around her. "Thank you! I know it's a lot to ask, but Francine seems completely at a loss as to what happened. The outside consultant is coming in tomorrow, and I'll be the first person he talks to. And we're all going to be questioned, even you."

Cara's muscles went rigid, and she backed out of the hug. "Even me?" Her voice came out high.

"I know. It's ridiculous. You aren't responsible for these accounts. I'm pretty sure, no matter what I do, I'm going to be fired for incompetence." DeeDee turned toward the door. "I appreciate you looking this over, though. Maybe you can find the mistake, and I can keep my job. Right now, I've got to make lasagna." She walked away.

"I'll...I'll do my best," Cara called after her, but even she could hear the uncertainty in her tone.

If she was questioned, if people started investigating her background, it wouldn't matter how many booklets she stapled.

Any hope she had for happiness here in Abundance would be gone.

Chapter Twelve

"Cyndi, I know you were ready to head home," Will said late Tuesday. "But I want to talk to you about taking on some bigger stories." He'd been watching for her most of the afternoon, but she'd been out on an interview. Luckily, he'd caught her when she popped in.

The intern put her enormous, tan purse on the floor and scooted forward in her chair, closer to his desk.

A positive sign, as if she was eager to make up for her last big story, the one she'd completely botched. No. He shouldn't think like that. He had to help her succeed, not just for the sake of the *News*, but because he was supposed to be teaching her about reporting in the real world.

"With Russell leaving, I'm going to ask you to cover a few of the regular meetings he's been handling." Will checked his wall calendar. "We've got three times a month when there are two important meetings on one night. I normally cover one, but I can't do both."

Cyndi's eyes grew wider, and she gave a short, jerky nod. "I can do this, Will. I know I messed things up before, but I'll do better."

A bit of the tension in his shoulders eased. See? This *could* work. "The first meeting is tomorrow night. I'll handle planning and zoning. I want you to cover the school board. It should be routine, but you never know."

She nodded again, so vigorously that her frizzy bangs bounced.

"Russell's already left to pack for his workshop, but check in his desk for a file on the school board. He should at least have old agendas that you can take home to read. Tomorrow, go through the back issues upstairs. The fourth Thursday of every month there should be a story on the school board's meeting the night before. Read the past three or four months and read last August. Most of what the school board does is cyclical."

"Okay," she said.

"I'm sure you'll do a great job."

"Thanks." She bounced up and hurried out the door.

Will watched her go. He must have sounded more confident than he felt.

He picked up the editorial he was writing. He'd read it one last time before he grabbed dinner and went to the park board meeting, a meeting that unfortunately would run about three hours. It always did, thanks to two board members who liked to hear themselves talk and a president who didn't stop them. Will would come in early tomorrow to write it up. By ten o'clock tonight, he would have had his fill for the day of being the editor of the local paper. He—

The fax machine on the side table let out a series of beeps, and a light on its side began to flash. He laid the editorial on the desk and got up to see what was coming in.

The cover sheet had a scribbled note from his buddy Andy over in Wichita. "Been out of town on vacation. Just got your message last night. Thought you might want to read this."

The bottom of the cover sheet slowly emerged.

It had been so long since Will had left a message at Andy's paper that he'd figured contacting him had been ridiculous. And he'd decided Cara must have been telling the truth about being from Illinois, especially after how she agreed with him about how destructive lies were. So what could this be?

The cover sheet dropped onto the tray, and the machine began to spit out the actual fax, a copy of a news article. Will bent his head sideways to read the page as it printed out.

"Accountant Daughter Questioned in Smith Investment Scam" the headline read. Two columns of text ran next to a photo of a woman who looked like Cara, only with lighter hair.

Will's gut churned as the rest of the page appeared.

Ten minutes later, he sat at his desk, rubbing his forehead as he read the two news articles Andy had sent. The more he read, the more his stomach burned.

There was no question. Cara Smith was actually Caroline Ann Smith, who had previously gone by Ann. And she wasn't from Illinois, she was from Spottsville, Kansas, exactly as he'd suspected.

Back in Spottsville, her father had built a company bilking retirees, many of them farmers with no pensions. Ann, who had worked in accounting at her father's company, had been questioned but never arrested.

His first instinct had been correct. She'd been lying to everyone in town.

Including him.

And now she worked at city hall where money might be missing.

This was who he was dating. Just the woman every man dreamed of.

Sweet, beautiful, and a scam artist.

Sure, the articles made it clear that Cara had never been charged, only questioned. And here in Abundance, she worked for Imogene, not for the treasurer. He shouldn't jump to conclusions. Certainly shouldn't run anything without verification.

But she'd lied. To him.

Anger shot through him, then froze into resolve.

She thought she could lie to him? He could handle that. In fact, he could probably handle it better than anyone in town. He scribbled a headline on a piece of scratch paper. Changed it a couple times until he came up with one he liked.

Investment Scammer's Daughter
Caught in City Hall Embezzlement

There, that nailed it. He pictured it. Two lines, 72 point type, all six columns across the top of the front page.

Talk about a story that would boost the *News'*

readership. This was the type of news that the wire services picked up, the type of story that won awards.

But what if it wasn't true?

Quickly, he wadded up the paper and tossed it in the trash.

Then he dug the phone book out of the drawer and dialed Russell at home.

No answer.

The conference didn't start until tomorrow. Knowing Russell, he was at the Wash 'n' Wear because he didn't have clean clothes to take to the conference.

Will tucked the fax pages under his phone to flatten them and picked up his notebook. He needed to grab dinner and get to the park board meeting.

He'd try Russell again later.

Cara had done her best to ignore it, but ever since her conversation with DeeDee, every nerve in her body was tensed, ready to flee.

We're all going to be questioned.

Cara sat on her couch, the words echoing in her brain.

She was going to be asked about missing money. Again.

Like that day back in Spottsville when the man with the badge said he needed to speak with her about irregularities in the books. When detectives had grilled her for hours.

But this was different. She wasn't responsible for the city's books. She spent her time answering the phone and filing. And, of course, stapling. She rubbed her right thumb over the heel of her left hand. Still sore.

Most likely, the problem was a mathematical error, not anything criminal.

Once Cara checked, she'd find the error, and everything would be solved. And she'd bring the files back to the office before anyone else got to work tomorrow. Probably, DeeDee would have been happier if Cara had read through them at city hall. But the place had cleared out quickly, until Cara's was the only car in the parking lot. And the building started making odd creaking noises, noises she never even noticed during the day with other people around. Far better to get up an hour early and study these at home than to wait around alone there until night fell.

She pulled a pen and a notepad from a kitchen drawer and sat down at the breakfast bar with DeeDee's papers. Then she got up again, poured a glass of water, and pulled a box of graham crackers and a jar of peanut butter out of the cabinet. Not what she'd planned to have for dinner, but she wasn't going to waste time cooking. She was going to find the error and put her mind at ease.

In fact... What would it hurt? Maybe God was listening. Maybe He did care.

She clasped her hands together as she'd seen people do when she was little and attended church with Mrs. Percer. Then she closed her eyes and bowed her head.

"God? If you're there, please help me. I really like it in Abundance. I don't want my life here to be ruined."

She didn't hear any answer, just a dog barking outside.

She opened her eyes. That was probably a total waste of time. Look how often she'd prayed for a family to no avail. She pulled the papers in front of her and began to read.

Hours later, she squeezed her eyes shut so tightly that after she opened them, she saw little spots of light. She'd been staring at the copied pages, some of which were fuzzy, for too long. And—surprise, surprise—God hadn't come through for her. She hadn't found a single mathematical error.

There was no way to avoid it.

She'd be questioned.

Again.

Her pulse beat out an uneven rhythm. Oh, she had nothing to worry about legally. She didn't have the necessary access to steal money from the city. But it wouldn't be long before the police figured out who she was.

Before the whole town heard.

Before she was right back in the same situation as in Spottsville.

What about Will?

Should she tell him the truth? Now, before everyone else found out? Was there a chance he might understand, might even help her with his position at the paper?

No. It would never work.

An ache built at the back of her throat. No matter how much she cared for him, no matter if she'd fallen a little bit in love with him, any dreams she had about Abundance were over. There was no way he'd want to date a woman whose father had stolen from pensioners. A woman who'd grown up with luxuries paid for with that stolen money. A woman trained in accounting who'd been too dumb to see what her father was doing.

Perhaps worst of all, a woman who'd lied to him.

That dishonesty was what she couldn't forgive in herself and what would destroy things with Will.

She hadn't lied about her feelings for him. She hadn't acted as if she cared for him and been seeing someone else.

She had simply lied about where she was from. And hidden who her family was.

In the eyes of the world that might not be a big deal. Some people would say she'd merely been discreet or would excuse her actions by saying she needed to know someone better before baring her past pain.

But the lie felt big to her. It had allowed her to hide so much.

And she was pretty sure that Will Hamlin, who placed such an emphasis on truth, would see her lie as unforgivable.

Cara got up from the breakfast bar, trudged into her bedroom, and pulled her typewriter from the back of the closet. Time to write a letter of resignation and repack her things.

Tomorrow she would drop her letter in the mail, leave the copied files on DeeDee's back porch, and get out of Abundance.

She could not—could not—relive the pain she'd gone through in Spottsville.

Not even for Will Hamlin.

Chapter Thirteen

Really? The cable guy was here too?

Cara ducked her head behind the trunk of her Volare and squeezed in one more box.

Who knew so many people would be in the parking lot of her apartment complex on a Wednesday morning? Every time she brought out another load, someone else was there.

The cable guy slammed the rear door of his big blue van and ambled past, whistling a tune from ABBA.

She shut her trunk, kept her head down, and hurried to her apartment.

With all the stuff she had to fit in the back seat, she probably had four more trips to make.

Then she'd be ready to take off. She'd already mailed her letter to Imogene. All she needed was for the apartment manager to arrive at work, find the note she'd left on his office door, and stop by her unit.

Cara stood for a moment inside her living room. Despite the all-avocado decorating style, she'd miss this place. And the rest of Abundance. Especially...

Her gaze fell on the basket of winter clothes that she'd never gotten the proper storage containers for. Her throat tightened, remembering how kind Will had been that night at the laundromat. The way he'd touched her face so gently...

She pressed her lips together. She was not going to cry.

If she had to leave, it was better to go now, before she'd bought furniture.

As if that mattered.

What she meant was that it was better to leave before she got more involved with Will.

She'd just have to find another nice town, another good job, another great guy.

Because she couldn't bear it if she had to look at rejection in his eyes. If he told her he didn't want to be involved with her. It was better to drive away with her few happy memories.

But...she didn't want another great guy. She wanted Will.

The whole situation was so unfair.

She drew in a shaky breath, picked up the next box, and—

Wait. Someone was knocking on her door. That had to be the manager.

Cara put the box down and opened the apartment door.

Two police officers stood on her front step.

The shorter one moved forward slightly, out of the sun

that had been gleaming on his dark hair. "Caroline Ann Smith?"

Her hand tightened on the doorknob. "Yes," she said, barely above a whisper.

"I'm Officer Thackery." He gestured to the younger man beside him. "This is Officer Blair."

The younger officer handed her some folded papers. "We have a warrant to search your apartment and your vehicle."

Cold sweat broke out all over Cara's body.

No.

No.

No!

She backed away and gulped for air.

Officer Thackery pulled on a pair of rubber gloves and walked into her living room.

Cara looked at the other officer, careful not to glance toward her breakfast bar at the papers DeeDee had given her.

Officer Blair stepped just inside and gestured to a stack of boxes near the door. "Are you moving in or moving out?"

"Uh, uh…" She looked up at him. He probably knew she worked at city hall. Probably knew exactly how long she'd been in town. But her plan to leave, which had made sense half an hour ago, made her look so, so guilty. "Uh, both."

"Both?"

"I haven't been here that long, but it just isn't going to work out."

"Look what we have here." Officer Thackery pulled a

set of keys from her purse, which was sitting on the couch. "Check out those plastic identifying bands, one on each key, arranged like a rainbow, exactly the way Francine described the missing key ring." He held it up for his partner to see. "The one with the green band, I think she said, is to that file cabinet she keeps locked in her office."

Cara's heart pounded. "I've never seen those keys. And I've never been in Francine's private office."

Officer Thackery dropped the keys into an evidence bag. The papers from DeeDee were in another clear bag that he had tucked under his arm.

"We're going to detain you, Miss Smith. We'd like you to come down to the station for questioning."

The walls of her apartment seemed to grow closer, like a trap shutting around her. She couldn't be taken down to the police station. Not here, where she had no fiscal authority over the missing money. Not now, when she was so close to leaving town. Not...

Not again.

This could not be happening to her again.

Three hours later, in an interview room at the Abundance Police station, Cara sat beside Stu Abbott, the only lawyer in town who was available. The police had read her Miranda rights and then repeatedly asked about those keys, about the files they'd found in her kitchen, and about why she'd been packing to leave town. And though neither officer mentioned it, from the way they acted, she'd bet they knew all about her past in Kansas.

Again and again, she'd told them she had nothing to

do with the theft at city hall. She'd explained that she was looking over the papers for a friend who was concerned about the missing money. And she'd denied any knowledge of those keys.

But where had the keys come from? Had someone she knew, someone she trusted, slipped in when she was in the copy room or the bathroom and put them in her purse to make her look guilty?

Officer Blair glanced at Officer Thackery.

Officer Thackery studied her, his mouth drawn in, his dark hair shining under the fluorescent lights.

Cara kept her eyes on his. She would not look down. If she did, she'd seem guilty. Surely, if she looked right at him, he would see the innocence in her eyes.

After what seemed like a week, Officer Thackery nodded.

Cara's pulse throbbed in her ears. She could feel droplets of sweat forming on her forehead. And she gripped the edge of the table so hard that her knuckles turned white. Because that nod wasn't a you're-free-to-go nod. It was a nod that meant he thought she was guilty, thought the case would hold up in court, thought she should be in jail.

She struggled for a breath. Her gaze shifted from the door to Stu to the officers. Then back to Stu, silently begging him to say or do something to save her.

But Stu sat silently as if her case was nothing more than another statistic in the sum of his failures.

This was horrible. Horrible. She should have never worked at city hall, never moved to Abundance, never stopped running.

Officer Blair rose to his feet. "Caroline Ann Smith," he said. "I'm placing you under arrest."

Will scanned the pasted-up front page of the Wednesday edition of *The Abundance News.* The layout was clean, the caption on the photo above the fold had been corrected, and no typos leapt out at him. "It's good to go," he said to Larry, one of the pressmen.

"Okay. Thanks." Larry took the page and headed downstairs, his work shoes thudding on the steps.

For the editorial department, it was another issue done.

Will returned to his office, just in time to take a call from his mom's friend, Lydia, who was phoning to complain that her paperboy had hit her gladioli when he tossed out yesterday's edition. Will listened politely, apologized, then routed her call to circulation and raised his eyes toward his office ceiling. He blew out a long breath and tried to relax his shoulder.

It didn't help. There was a kink in there that came from holding the phone with his shoulder while he listened to people complain. A kink that lingered, much like the feeling—now that he was over his initial anger—that he should give Cara a chance to explain.

Of course, that feeling might spring from his foolish heart and not his journalist's instinct. Or from his own ego, wanting to prove that he wasn't stupid enough to be fooled by a scammer, but still...

This morning had been insane. On top of hammering out his article about the park board and his regular editing duties, he'd had to completely rewrite Cyndi's school board story. He'd wanted to call Cara but hadn't had a minute to spare. And he'd never gotten ahold of Russell. Even this morning, there had been no answer and—

Hold on. Had he really left his phone at that angle last night when he put the faxes under it?

No, definitely not. He'd positioned the phone to cover the photo with Cara's face, which was now mostly visible.

He grabbed the fax pages and buried them out of sight in a desk drawer.

Had someone else read them? Should he ask his staff? Would they think he didn't trust them?

He shoved back his chair and stood up. If he didn't get an answer, he'd never be able to focus this afternoon. He'd better ask now before everyone dashed out to get lunch.

In the newsroom, Cyndi was already headed toward the door, hitching up the strap of her giant tan purse.

Will held out a hand to catch her attention. "Hey, wait. I have a question."

Cyndi stopped and propped one arm on the reception counter.

"Did, um…" This was going to sound idiotic. Insulting. But… "Did any of you go in my office last night?"

Velma shook her head.

"Nah," Kirk said. "I've swiped napkins from your desk drawer in the past, but not last night."

Cyndi pulled her purse in front of her like a shield.

"Cyndi?"

She shrank back.

"We need to talk." He pointed toward his office.

She took a couple of slow steps in that direction.

He gestured for her to go ahead, followed her in, and shut the door.

She sat down with her big purse squarely across her lap.

Will went around his desk to his chair. "Well...?"

"It was me. I...I came back to the paper last night to read the back issues about the school board. I was opening a package of Smarties, and as I walked by your office, I spilled them. Some of them rolled under the door. When I went in to pick them up, I saw those faxes." Her chin jutted out. "They were right out there in plain sight."

"They were almost completely covered by my phone," Will said. "For a reason." The girl was a waste in the newsroom, incapable of writing the simplest of stories, and now she had violated his privacy. Hal had never locked his office. Will never even considered it. Apparently, with an intern like Cyndi, it was necessary.

"Well, I read them," she said.

He crossed his arms and glared at her. She didn't even sound as if she felt guilty. She sounded indignant.

"And I told my Aunt Imogene," Cyndi said.

Every nerve in Will's body jolted as though he'd been hit with a current. "You what?"

"She has a right to know. I can't believe you were sitting on that information, letting a thief work in the mayor's office simply because you think she's cute."

Heat poured into Will's chest. His pulse throbbed in his temples, and he dug his fingers into the armrests of his chair to keep from reaching across the desk and throttling her.

The presumptuous little fool didn't understand the

difference between when a suspect was questioned and when they were charged. She'd violated the privacy of his office. And she'd ignored his authority.

Yes, there was a chance that Cyndi was right, that Cara was an embezzler. But in those news stories from Kansas, Cara had never been arrested, only questioned. She might have been entirely innocent back then. And, though he'd been suspicious of her at first, after he'd thought about it, his gut told him she was innocent now.

Look at how she'd been eager to help the families who lost everything in the fire. That didn't sound like a person who would steal from others. And at the picnic, she'd talked about Abundance as if she liked the town, cared about it.

No, the idea of her stealing from the city didn't fit.

Besides, any decision about what to do with the information Andy had faxed should have been made by Will. Not by a snoopy, self-righteous college sophomore who didn't even understand the inverted-pyramid style of writing a news story, much less fair reporting.

Someone pounded on his door.

"Later," he yelled.

"Will, you've got a phone call," Kirk said as he opened the door a crack.

A phone call? Kirk was interrupting him for a phone call? "Take a message," Will bellowed. "And shut the door."

Kirk did.

Will looked back at Cyndi. What was he going to do? Without her, once Russell left, he'd be the entire news staff. One person. To handle everything.

But was she actually helping?

No. She wasn't. Look at that mess she'd made of the school board story.

"Go home," he said to Cyndi. "Take your things."

"You're firing me?" Her voice rose, ending with a squeak.

"I am. I don't want an intern I can't trust."

Cyndi's mouth fell open, then she stomped out and slammed the door.

Good riddance. Imogene would be furious, but he didn't care.

Will grabbed the phone and dialed Cara at work.

"Mayor Findley."

Imogene? The last person he wanted to talk to. Should he tell her what he'd just done? No. Cyndi needed to grow up, and part of growing up was learning to own up to failure. Let her take the brunt of Imogene's response. Besides, Cara was what mattered now. "Hi, Imogene. This is Will Hamlin. May I speak with Cara?"

Silence filled the line, then Imogene replied, her voice tight. "Cara isn't in today. Can I help you, Will?"

"Will!" Kirk was banging on the door again, this time so loudly that there must be a fire in the pressroom.

"Thank you, no," Will said into the phone, and he hung up. "What?" he shouted at the door.

Kirk flung it open. "That phone call was an anonymous source. A woman who said she'd been talking with Russell and can't get ahold of him. But the story he was working on, about money missing at city hall, just broke wide open. They've arrested Cara Smith."

Chapter Fourteen

Cara sat on the cot in the corner of her jail cell late Wednesday afternoon, her back propped against the wall.

Everything around her was gray—gray walls, gray floor, gray blanket. Everything except the black metal bars that held her in.

And she was so alone, the only person in the whole police station basement from what she could tell. No drunk in the next cell being held after a bar fight, no guard to check on her. Just her and the cold, damp air and the concrete floor and walls that echoed back the slightest sound.

All she'd wanted was a chance to start over, to begin a new life in a place where people wouldn't judge her based on her father's crimes. She'd tried to build that new life.

And failed.

She'd never be in this cell if Dad hadn't done what he did.

Wasn't a father supposed to care for his children, supposed to provide good things for them? Not her father. No, he'd betrayed every bit of love and faith she'd placed in him. Sure, he'd provided her with material things, but those things had meant more to him than to her. She'd never asked for the fancy car or for the new house he'd built when she was in high school. And he'd made people in Spottsville hate her.

Here in Abundance? Well, she could see that she'd made herself look guilty by taking those files home and by deciding to leave town, but the police had clearly connected her to her father. That had to have affected their judgment of her. And if Dad's actions hadn't made her go through such misery back in Spottsville, she might have bravely faced the situation at city hall instead of wanting to run.

So, yes, part of this mess was her fault. Part of it was the fault of whoever stole the money from the city. And part of the blame—a large part—went to her father.

But allocating blame wasn't helping. The real question was what to do now.

She certainly wasn't going to waste any time praying. God didn't listen, no matter what DeeDee said. Maybe he cared about other people and answered their prayers. But Cara had prayed, asking for help and telling God that she didn't want her life here in Abundance ruined.

The next morning she'd been arrested.

How much more ruined could her life be?

She shrank into the corner, pulled her feet closer on the cot, and wrapped her arms around her knees. An ache spread through her chest, and she scrunched herself into a ball, squeezing her eyes shut. If only she could open them and learn this was all just a bad dream.

She opened one eye, then the other. It wasn't a bad dream.

It was real.

But she was innocent! She hadn't stolen a penny.

Somehow, some way, she had to prove that.

A better lawyer, that was the first thing. Stu Abbott was a joke. She'd contact Dad's lawyer and ask him to suggest someone.

Even if they convicted her, she'd keep appealing until she was free.

And then she'd begin again. She'd made a mistake moving only one state away, but there was always Mexico. She'd taken Spanish in high school. Or she could go somewhere in South America. Or even Spain. She'd find a way—once again—to start over and hide her past forever.

Cara. Arrested.

Will couldn't even put the two words in the same sentence. He looked across his desk at Kirk. "Did the woman on the phone say anything else?"

"No. I tried to get more out of her, and I tried to get a number or get her to say she'd call back, but she hung up."

"Okay." Will ran a hand through his hair. "Thanks for talking with her. I was…"

"You were dealing with Cyndi," Kirk said. He grunted and walked away.

Will stared out the door after him. What did he do now?

True, there was a chance Cara might have been involved in criminal activity in Kansas. The investigators might not have had enough evidence to arrest her. If so, she might be the person who'd stolen money here in Abundance. The timing was definitely suspicious.

But the police might very well be investigating her because he'd dug into her past, because Cyndi gave Andy's information to Imogene, and because Imogene passed it on to the authorities.

What if Cara was innocent? What if he'd only learned part of the story? That meant that once again his misinformation had led to someone's misery. It wasn't as bad as passing on a lie that caused someone to kill themselves, but still… What a disaster!

So what was the right thing to do?

Even if he got *All the President's Men* off the shelf and flipped through every page, the answer wasn't there. Should he call Hal and ask him what to do? No, he and his wife were on a two-month RV vacation out West. Dad? No, Dad hadn't taken classes in journalism ethics, and he didn't know Cara the way Will did.

What was the answer? How was he going to figure this out?

At last, he bowed his head and prayed.

Half an hour later, Will followed Officer Brent Adams down the basement hall at the police station.

Will, Kirk, and Velma had discussed the situation and agreed that the most ethical thing was for someone other than Will to cover the story. Until Russell got back that someone would be Velma. She hadn't written a news story in years, but she still could.

This left Will free to do what his gut or his conscience or possibly even God had told him to do—check on Cara and apologize. He could never fix the role he'd played in his friend's death in high school. But he could try to fix this. And, thanks to the fact that he'd known Brent Adams since third grade, he could take the first step, apologizing.

"She's down this hall," Brent said.

"I appreciate this, Brent." Will had been in the basement of the police station before, even interviewed a prisoner down here, but he'd never noticed the hollow clanking of the pipes, the hard gray of the walls and floor, or the harsh smell of disinfectant that hung in the air. Poor Cara!

Will and Brent rounded a corner.

There she was, sitting on the cot in her cell with her head hanging down.

Will moved closer and gripped the bars of the cell. The chill from the metal spread up his arms and into his heart. She looked pale and fragile and vulnerable. How could they have put her in here? "Cara?"

She jumped up and rushed toward him, clasping his hands. "Oh, thank you for coming to see me. I can't believe I'm in here." She sucked in a breath.

"Of course I came. As soon as I heard." The poor girl. Her hands were icy. Why didn't the police turn back the AC a bit?

"I had almost given up hope," she said. "But I should have known I could count on you. Oh, Will"—her voice caught, and her eyes shone—"you have to believe me. I

137

didn't have anything to do with the theft from the city."

A lump rose in his throat, and he tried to swallow it away. But his guilt didn't disappear that easily. It was so obvious she was innocent. So obvious there had been a mistake. "I believe you, Cara, but...you need to know something."

"What? Is there news?" She squeezed his hands. "Have they figured out what really happened to the money?"

"I think..." Will made another attempt to swallow the lump in his throat. She was never going to forgive him. No, it wasn't simply that she wouldn't forgive him. She would *hate* him. But he had to get it over with. "I think I'm the reason you were arrested."

She dropped his hands and jolted back. "What?"

"I checked into your background. I found out about your dad and how you were questioned."

Her mouth fell open. Her eyes grew wide, and the irises seemed to darken.

"I had faxes of news articles about you on my desk, and the intern at the paper saw them and told her aunt—Imogene."

"You what?" Cara's breath came faster, and her chest heaved. Then her voice came out harsher, and she enunciated every letter sharply. "What was it you said? 'I never, ever want to destroy an innocent person's life with a lie.'"

"Cara, I—"

"I thought I could start over if I moved to a place where people had never heard of my father. I thought a town named Abundance would be perfect. Too bad I got involved with a *reporter*." She spoke the word in the same tone one might use to say *serial killer.*

Brent took a step toward them.

"I'd barely met you when I decided to check up on you," Will said, grabbing the cell bars. "I thought I was doing the right thing. I mean, I knew you were hiding something when I saw that bumper sticker on your car. I've been to Erlene's Bait and Pizza."

"So if you'd never talked to me at the diner," she said, her words pelting him, "if you'd never pretended to be nice, never walked me back to the office, none of this would have happened?"

Heat poured into Will's chest. "This is not all my fault," he said, louder than he meant to. "You were the one who was lying."

"I only lied about one thing," she spat out. "Where I was from. If a town had treated you the way Spottsville treated me, you'd lie to get away from it too. But you—you hurt me, just as much as my father did. Sneaking around, digging into my past." Her hands trembled at her sides, and her eyes shone with unshed tears. "Couldn't you have trusted me enough to ask me about it?"

"I was going to but—"

Cara thrust her hands on her hips, and two red patches appeared on her pale cheeks. "Like I believe a word you're saying," she shouted. "Leave me alone!"

"Cara, I—"

Brent took hold of Will's elbow and pulled him away. "Buddy, you're gonna have to leave."

Will wrenched his arm free. "No! I've got to make her understand."

Brent's eyes hardened, and he took a firmer grip on

Will's elbow. "Not if it means I lose my job. C'mon, you're going."

"But—"

A metallic *clunk* echoed from the far end of the hall as if the door there had fallen shut.

Brent's gaze darted toward the sound, and he yanked on Will's arm.

"Brent—" Will planted his feet. He couldn't leave Cara like this.

Brent shook his head, and his eyes held a silent message that Will needed to shut up. And that he was asking too much from his old friend.

Pain dug at the back of Will's throat, and an ache sliced through his chest. No matter how much he wanted to explain things to Cara, he couldn't endanger Brent's job.

Will looked back toward the cell and drew in a ragged breath. Then he stiffly walked with Brent toward the door at the other end of the hall.

After ten or fifteen steps, Will heard Cara sobbing.

His stomach tightened into an unyielding knot.

How had this happened again? How had he, who wanted more than anything else to uncover truth, been the source of a lie that was destroying someone's life?

He'd been responsible for Gary's death.

And now he was responsible for Cara's arrest.

Chapter Fifteen

Will slammed Russell's bottom desk drawer shut.

Velma glanced up from her typewriter. "Nothing?"

"Not a single file on the money that's missing." He'd been searching ever since he got back from seeing Cara.

"I told you there wasn't. I even scanned through the two most recent notebooks from the top drawer." Lines deepened at the corners of her mouth. "Not a word. At least not from what I could read."

"Your article for tomorrow should be fairly easy," Will said. "Straight-forward reporting about the fact that the money is missing, with quotes from the cops. But if you're going to write a decent follow-up for the Friday paper—"

"And," Velma said, "if you're going to try to figure out if the police are wrong, if someone other than Cara is the embezzler—"

"We need more info." Will shoved the chair back from Russell's desk and stood.

Velma bit at her thumbnail. "I'm not sure how…"

"I know you're interviewing someone for a feature tonight. But Russell's got to have those files from his anonymous source somewhere," Will said. "If I have to drive to Columbia to get them, I will." He checked his watch. It was already close to seven. "But first I've got to figure out how to get ahold of him. I'll start calling hotels." Will turned toward his office.

"His expenses are paid by that paper in Florida," Velma called out.

Will looked back. "So I should start with the expensive places?"

"That's where I'd stay."

She was right. A swift check of the Columbia phone book and a few calls to the priciest-sounding hotels was all it took. At the third hotel Will tried, the front desk connected him to the room of Mr. Russell Johnston.

Twenty minutes later Will found a spare key right where Russell said it would be, under a chunk of grayish-white rock near his apartment door.

Will let himself into the apartment, which was about the same as it had been last month when he and Russell had watched a ball game on TV. No testimony to tidiness, that was for sure. There was an odd odor, like Chinese food left in the trash for days. And Will wasn't certain, but when he turned on the light, he thought he saw a roach racing to hide.

But right there in the middle of the round kitchen table was a notebook and a stack of papers, the ones Russell had gotten from his anonymous inside source.

Yes! Will sat down and opened the notebook. He could

take it back to the office to read, but he'd rather know now.

But the notebook didn't have much. A few vague quotes. Scribbles that Will wasn't able to decipher. Big block letters, underlined, that said NOT FOR ATTRIBUTION.

He closed the notebook and thumbed through the papers underneath, peering at the numbers and the names of various accounts.

It was no use.

None of it made sense.

What was he going to do? Russell had said on the phone that he was stumped and had no way to initiate contact with his source.

Will's stomach cramped like the time he'd eaten under-cooked chicken at that sports bar in St. Louis. If Cara's attorney didn't find a way to prevent it, she could go to jail for years. Her life would be ruined. All because of him. He needed to figure this out. How was he going to do that if he didn't understand finance? He needed help. He needed...

Dad.

"Plug this in under the sideboard, would you?" Dad held the cord for the adding machine toward Will.

That, at least, Will could handle. Figuring out what was going on with the city's books? Doubtful.

He and Dad had been sitting at his folks' dining room table and going through Russell's papers for the past forty minutes, and Will hadn't noticed anything suspicious. Most likely, he never would. Sure, he balanced his own checkbook every month. The math was easy for numbers that small. This enormous tangle, with money coming into so many accounts and out of so many others, made his head throb.

And asking Dad to help him, well, that made him feel even more stupid. But Dad had a head for figures. Will wasn't letting his pride keep him from fixing this disaster. Cara was not going to prison, not if he could help it.

At least Dad hadn't commented on Will's failings. He'd listened to the story about Cyndi and agreed when Will said he thought Cara was innocent. "Your mother really liked her," he'd said. "And she's got a good sense about people." Then he'd sat down at the big oak dining room table with the papers Will had brought. A few minutes later, he left to get two legal pads, pencils, and his ancient adding machine, the one he used every month to do the books for the farm.

Dad adjusted his glasses and turned on the adding machine, then began reading a handful of pages and making notes on his pad.

Will picked up the remaining pages and stretched his back against the oak dining room chair. Maybe he could at least understand the overall picture of the city's money. Somewhere there had been a report that listed all the accounts. He pulled the stack toward him and started digging.

Across the table, the adding machine hummed, giving an agitated *ching* every few seconds when Dad hit the Total button. Will knew that sound quite well. One day when he was a kid, he'd hit Total again and again and again, until Mom told him to quit wasting the machine's roll of paper.

"Humph." Dad pulled off his glasses and rubbed behind one ear.

"Anything?" Will moved his chair closer to the table.

"No. Everything balances and seems reasonable."

Will returned to reading.

About twenty minutes later, a car door slammed outside. In the driveway, a tan Chevy Nova sat under the maple tree.

"It must be someone to see your mother." Dad put his glasses back on. "Let's keep searching."

"Look who's here to help." Mom walked in and tipped her head toward the guest behind her.

It was DeeDee McAlister, holding a stack of papers.

"Mary called and said you were trying to help Cara. I...well, I went back into the office, and I copied all the files from the past six months that I could find. Francine's the best boss in the whole world, but there must be something she's not seeing. There's no way Cara Smith stole money from Abundance."

"DeeDee," Mom said. "You could get fired."

"If I hadn't given Cara copies of those ledger pages and statements the other day, she would never be in jail. I tried to tell the police that I'd given her things to look over since she's so good at accounting, but Francine talked right over me, and the police didn't hear what I was saying. I mean, I know Francine was trying to protect me because I probably shouldn't have given those files to Cara, but the police think Cara has them because she was stealing from the city." She dumped her papers on the table. "I had to do something to help."

Mom's brow furrowed. "But DeeDee—"

"No one at work will ever know. I was alone in the building, and I put everything back where I found it."

Mom gave DeeDee a you-know-better frown and headed toward the kitchen. "I guess I'll leave you all to figure this out."

"Mary said you have some documents already?" DeeDee sat down at the table.

"From anonymous source," Will said.

"I bet that was Rachel. It seems like something she'd do." DeeDee flipped through the pages on the table. "Anyway, some of what I brought may be copies of the same things."

"Will, why don't you sort them," Dad said. "If you find something we don't have, pass it over to DeeDee and me."

"Okay." Sorting, yeah, that was about his skill level. But at least he could do something.

Many of the documents were in fact things he and Dad had already seen. He added several bank statements to the pile of duplicates.

But the next sheet...

Will scratched the side of his head. "Abundance has an account in Millersburg?"

"No, we do all our banking in Abundance," DeeDee said. "I think it's required by city ordinance."

Will held up a bank statement. "But this Reserve Capital Improvements Account—"

"Hold on." Dad thumbed through the papers in front of him. "I have the statement for the Reserve Capital Improvements Account right here. It's in the First Bank of Abundance. It had deposits coming in through May."

Goosebumps sprang up on Will's arms, and he drew in

a quick breath. "That's when the first deposit was made in this account," he said. "In Millersburg. And every month, shortly after it's deposited, the money is taken out."

For a second, no one spoke. Will looked from Dad to DeeDee and back again.

"I've never heard of an account over in Millersburg." DeeDee sounded baffled. "Ever."

"Will, when was the first activity on that statement?" Dad said.

Will checked the statement. "June 7th of this year."

"So there's the real account, at the bank here in Abundance where the money should be going." DeeDee held one hand out, palm up. "And there's an account over in Millersburg with the same name." She held out her other hand. "Where somebody is funneling money and then stealing it from our town?"

Dad frowned and nodded slowly. "That's what it sure seems like to me. I'd guess someone set up an account over there with themselves as the only signatory. The city books look normal until someone notices that the account in Abundance isn't building up the way it should."

"And that isn't an account we use much," DeeDee said. "It makes sense that no one noticed it for a while."

Will's pulse picked up. "Cara didn't move here until August. There's no way she set up a bank account back in June." And no way she should be in jail.

"No." DeeDee's throat tensed as if she'd swallowed hard. "Pretty much the only person who could have opened that other account is Francine."

147

At the far end of the basement hall at the police station, a door opened with a creak.

Cara scrambled up from her cot and rushed toward the bars of her jail cell. Was it someone about her bail? Please, please let it be about her bail. She never wanted to spend another night behind bars.

Ever.

Physically, it was wretched. She'd been cold and, after a night of tossing and turning, sat up this morning as achy as if she had the flu. Emotionally, it was worse. All night, her mind had been like a cassette tape that someone kept flipping over and over, hitting Play again and again, repeating every awful story she'd ever heard about being a woman in prison.

"Looks like today is your lucky day," the officer said as he came down the hall.

"My bail?"

"Even better," he said. "You're free to go. All charges have been dropped."

Cara's legs wobbled, and she reached for the metal bars to steady herself. "How?"

"It's that—what do they call it?—investigative journalism."

"A reporter helped me?"

"That Will Hamlin, the guy you were yelling at the other day. He ferreted out information that changed the whole case and started calling people before seven this morning. I guess it helps to be friends with a reporter. Especially if he's got it bad for you." The officer unlocked the cell and swung the door open.

"I can't believe it," she said, breathless. She was free.

With each step she followed him down the hall, adrenaline tingled through her veins, and she felt more like herself. Being released from jail was a like a whopping injection of antibiotics, coursing through her system and curing her despair.

A few minutes later, she walked out of the police station. Never had the plain storefronts of downtown Abundance been more beautiful or the late August heat as welcome. She closed her eyes and faced the sun, letting the warmth soak into her arms and shoulders, melting away the cold from that basement cell. Then she turned and—

"Hey." Will stood before her.

She jerked back, her chest suddenly hot. Maybe the guard was right, and Will had gotten her free. And maybe she should feel grateful. But she didn't. She glared at him.

"Dad, DeeDee, and I figured it out. Francine is the thief. Not you."

Cara's breath grew shallow. Francine certainly could have embezzled the money and planted those keys in her purse to pin the crime on her, the new girl in town, thinking she'd be easier to suspect of a crime. And then when Cara had taken those files home, she'd unknowingly made Francine's accusation even more credible. But Francine had been so kind to her, to everyone... "Really? The woman the whole town loves?"

"The police are bringing her in right now." Pride rang in Will's voice.

Exactly what she'd expect. Pride. A big scoop for the journalist. Something for the front page. He might even want a quote from her. She pressed her lips shut. Not. Happening.

"I thought you might need a ride to your apartment." He gave her an eager, everything's-just-fine-between-us smile.

Everything most definitely wasn't fine. He was freshly shaved and showered, wearing khakis and a blue button-down. Her face was greasy, and her hair hung limp. Her eyes probably had dark circles under them. And she smelled like Eau de Jail.

"I'd rather walk." It had to be less than three miles to her apartment. A hike, but better than being around someone she didn't trust.

"Please, can I talk to you for a minute? Over there? I want to apologize." He angled his head toward a bench a half a block away.

She glanced at it.

No amount of groveling could make up for what he'd done, but she'd let him try. Perhaps she owed him that much. "I guess." He could say what he wanted, then she'd leave him there, apology not accepted, and walk home.

He held one hand toward the bench and brought the other toward her arm.

She pulled it close to her side, out of his reach, and walked briskly ahead. Then she sat. Apologize all you want to, Will Hamlin.

He lowered himself to the bench, spread his hands on his legs, and leaned toward her. "I'm sorry you got arrested because I checked into your past. I was trying to wrap my brain around what I read in those news articles. Even without talking to you, I knew in my gut that you weren't a thief."

A tingle shot through her, and her eyes pricked. He

knew she wasn't a thief. He *knew*. He believed in her...

She blinked and crossed her arms, walling off that tingle. Nice words, but they didn't explain why he'd exposed her past.

"I was going to ask you about what happened as soon as the paper was out yesterday. I had just approved the last page when I realized the things on my desk had been moved. Even though I had the faxes covered, Cyndi had been snooping in my office, and she told Imogene what she found. I fired her, but the damage was already done."

"You fired Cyndi?"

"Yeah."

Cara sat up a little taller.

"Then my dad and I went through documents that Russell got from an anonymous source about the missing money. DeeDee brought over more documents, and the three of us worked it out." Will hesitated. "Can you ever forgive me?"

Cara's breath caught. She looked him hard in the eyes, then turned away, her arms still crossed, her hands tucked in, and her lower lip bit between her teeth. Last night had been so, so awful, and her plan to start over in Abundance was ruined. All because Will had snuck around looking into her past.

But what Cyndi had done wasn't his fault.

And he'd believed in her. What she wouldn't have given back in Spottsville for one person—just one person— to have believed in her. To have tried to help her even a little.

So could she forgive him?

Yes.

She turned back to him, her hands falling to her sides. "I can. I forgive you."

He let out a ragged breath. "Thank you."

But she still didn't understand one thing. "I can't believe you and your dad and DeeDee helped me get out of jail. Back in Spottsville, once people knew about my dad, they hated me. That's why I left. And why I tried so hard to hide any ties to my past when I moved here."

"Maybe the people your dad took money from had to take their anger out on someone. I'm sorry that was you. You're not responsible for what he did."

Her throat went raw and the tears she'd held back poured down her cheeks. She slumped on the bench, the wires that had kept her upright all these months suddenly pulled from her frame. "It...it means an awful lot to have you say that." Her words came out shaky and low, too weak to convey how much his support meant, how it eased not just the pain of the past twenty-four hours, but even part of the pain she'd gone through in Spottsville, pain she'd thought she'd carry for the rest of her life.

She brushed the tears from her cheeks. "I should have told you about my dad earlier. I was going to. I just had to get up the courage."

He squeezed her shoulders, then dropped his arm to his side and glanced down. "There's something I need to tell you."

"What?"

"I've been a huge hypocrite. Because I have something from my past that I've never told anyone."

She wiped away a final tear and turned to face him more fully. "You do? What is it?"

A shudder went through him. A moment later, he cleared his throat. "Back when I was in high school, I was best friends with a guy named Gary Edwards. One day I heard that his girlfriend was cheating on him. I...thought he should know." Will rubbed the back of his neck. "After I told Gary what I'd heard, he drove his car into a tree." Will's shoulders sank, and he stared at the sidewalk. "They said it was an accident, but I always thought it was suicide."

How horrible. She rested a hand on his arm. "You were doing the right thing. You couldn't have known what he would do."

Will looked up, his hazel eyes filled with guilt and pain and sadness. "But the story about his girlfriend wasn't even true. I learned later it was just a rumor. And I've never told anyone the part I played, not even his parents. I tried once, but... Anyway, your lie, about where you were from, is nothing compared to what I did." His shoulders sank even lower.

The raw feeling returned to Cara's throat, the ache spreading into her chest. Poor Will. He'd been carrying this burden for so long. "How old were you?"

"Seventeen," he mumbled.

"You probably didn't even consider the possibility that he might kill himself. You need to forgive yourself. And you need to tell his parents. They deserve to hear the truth, and I bet they'd forgive you."

He glanced up again. "You really think so?"

"I really do," she said, as convincingly as she could, and she squeezed his arm. "You were a kid. You were trying to help him."

The anguish faded from his eyes, and he took her hand, "I'm so glad you moved here." He gazed at her tenderly, as if he didn't care that her hair was a mess or that she smelled like a jail cell or that her father was a convicted conman.

Her chest eased and filled with warmth, even more wonderful than the August sun. He cared about her, truly cared about her, despite what her dad had done. "I'm glad I moved here too. I hope...I hope it works out." Maybe it could. "Do you think the people in Abundance can like me in spite of my father?"

"I think, Caroline Ann Smith, that most of Abundance can like you just fine." He turned to face her directly, and his voice grew more serious. "One guy, in particular, might even like you so much that if people around here don't see how great you are, and you want to move somewhere else, he'd move there too, just to be near you."

Her heart sped, and she gripped his hand more tightly.

Then that one guy in particular leaned forward and kissed her.

Chapter Sixteen

Cara stopped halfway up the stairs to the second floor of city hall and looked down toward the landing. Even though she'd given herself a pep talk at breakfast, the thought of heading right back down those stairs sounded awfully good. But if she wanted her job back, she couldn't run away.

It was Friday morning. Two days ago, she'd mailed a letter of resignation that Imogene should have already received. And was probably more than grateful for. After all, what boss wanted an employee who lied to her? Even if she had been innocent of the embezzlement?

But Cara had to ask. After a long shower once she got home from jail yesterday, she'd called Imogene's direct office line, but got no answer. She didn't want to leave a message. So she lay down for a quick nap—and ended up sleeping past five. She considered calling Imogene at home but decided it was better to go in, talk to her in person, and ask for her job back. Running away again wasn't what she wanted. Even if she was afraid of the town's judgment, she wanted to make things work here.

After yesterday, that seemed possible. She'd even gone to a hair salon last night and had her hair highlighted so she would be blonder and feel more like herself. Mostly, though, she was hopeful because of Will. He'd gotten her out of jail, and their relationship held real promise.

Was that what DeeDee meant when she said that sometimes God answered prayers in unexpected ways? Instead of helping her find the missing money, had God sent Will to find it?

She wasn't sure. But if God did hear her prayers, she shouldn't waste the opportunity.

She glanced around. The stairwell was empty. Quickly, she bowed her head and whispered. "Dear God, if it was you, thank you for sending Will to get me out of jail. And thank you for the nice lady at the hair salon who fit me in yesterday. And if there's any way, please help me be able to keep working here. Let Imogene give me my job back. And help me be brave."

She opened her eyes. She felt...well, not a lot different. The fear that she might not be rehired was still there.

But she had to try.

She raised her chin, climbed up the last few stairs, and stepped into the office.

There was her desk, right by the place where the sunbeam came through the windows in the afternoon, shining strong and steady on the old tile floor. Her chair, adjusted to the perfect height. Her spot, where she had been a part of this town, where she had thought she could contribute to making Abundance a good place to live. For that short time, she had fit in. If only she could again.

"Cara." DeeDee stood in the side doorway to the city treasurer's office as if her sensible, low, black heels had been fused to the floor. Then she rushed toward Cara and hugged her. "I'm so glad you're back!"

A tender ache filled Cara's chest. One more reason to hope things could work out in Abundance—DeeDee, a real friend. "Apparently, thanks in no small part to you," Cara whispered.

DeeDee's eyes widened, and she laid a finger over her lips, then turned her head toward Imogene's office. "Imogene, Cara's here."

"I wasn't expecting you," DeeDee said. "Imogene said she was going to call and tell you to take the day off."

Cara's stomach grew jittery, and she glanced toward Imogene's door. After she got three calls from reporters back in Kansas, who'd somehow heard she'd been in jail, she'd stopped answering her phone. She never dreamed Imogene would call. But her boss wouldn't have wanted to give her the day off if she'd accepted Cara's resignation, would she?

"I never got ahold of her," Imogene said as she came out of her office and patted Cara's back. "You poor thing. I'm so glad you're here. And I'm terribly sorry for what you went through. When the police questioned me, I felt I had to tell them about the articles Cyndi read. I should have trusted my gut. I knew you didn't steal anything."

Cara's stomach eased, and she let out a huge breath. Imogene believed in her. "I'm the one who should apologize," Cara said. "I should have been more honest with you about my past."

"But you had to spend a night in jail," DeeDee said. "It wasn't right. The police should have figured things out." She shook her head emphatically. "It's a good thing I—uh—it's a good thing Will Hamlin wanted to help you." She gestured toward Cara's hair. "I must say, after all you've been through, you look fabulous."

Cara raised a hand to her hair. "I wanted to be more my real self when I came to ask if I could still work here."

"Of course you can still work here," Imogene said. "We know you didn't steal from the city, and we don't care what your father did."

Cara's throat thickened. Imogene. DeeDee. And Will. Three people who didn't judge her based on her dad. And she had her job back. Everything she had prayed for—and more. "Thank you, thank you so much," she said to Imogene.

Imogene brushed Cara's words aside. "No need to thank me. We're lucky to have you here. Now, do you still want to be called Cara? You used to go by Ann, right?"

"I did." Cara paused, recalling the woman she used to be. "But Ann Smith had gotten too cynical, believing the worst of everyone. As Cara, I tried to have a more positive attitude. I want to stay Cara."

Imogene beamed. "You'll need that good attitude once you see the pile of work I've got waiting for you. Are you sure you don't want the day off?"

"Oh, no," Cara said. "I'd love to get back to work."

Imogene nodded. "All right, but first, we need to celebrate the fact that you're back. I've got a phone call to make, but why don't you pick up cinnamon rolls at the diner. My treat." She disappeared into her office, then returned, holding out a ten-dollar bill.

"I, uh..." Cara didn't reach for the money. Her breakfast pep talk wasn't enough to prepare her for a diner full of people.

"I'll go with you." DeeDee grabbed the bill from Imogene and put a hand on Cara's back, gently propelling her toward the door.

Buoyed by DeeDee's energy, Cara made it down the stairs. But outside on the sidewalk, she stopped. She'd already talked to Imogene. Wasn't one brave action enough for the day? She could picture people in the diner stopping, forks halfway to their mouths, to stare at her when she walked in. "I don't think I can do this. Everyone in there will be gossiping about me." She should wait a day or two. Or a week. Give herself time to prepare.

"We'll go in together. There will be talk, but the sooner you deal with it, the better." DeeDee slid an arm around Cara's waist and pulled her to her side.

Cara let out a shaky breath. Maybe she'd never be any more prepared than she was now. Maybe she needed to take this chance to see if she could make it here in Abundance, to see if she could be brave. "Might as well get it over with. Let everyone get a good look at the woman whose father's a con man."

"Remember, no matter what your father did, you have another father, a heavenly father who loves you."

An odd tingle ran through Cara's chest, and she looked over at DeeDee. She'd prayed about her job. A minute later, Imogene had welcomed her back, and now DeeDee was telling her that God loved her. Was that a coincidence?

It didn't feel like a coincidence. It felt like a nudge. "You know," she said. "I'm beginning to see that."

"Good."

Cara straightened her shoulders and took the first steps toward Cassidy's. A few minutes later, DeeDee opened the diner door.

A collective awareness rippled through the bacon-scented air, and every eye turned toward Cara.

Just as quickly, everyone turned away and resumed their conversations.

Cara backed toward the door, her mind swirling with memories of similar reactions from people in Spottsville.

No wonder she hadn't wanted to come to the diner. And no wonder she'd felt she had to lie when she moved to Abundance.

And then, in a flash, another similarity struck her.

She was just like her father.

He'd grown up poor and based his whole self-worth on money. He only began conning people after some of his investments tanked, trying to hold on to the symbols of wealth he'd accumulated.

He'd used lies to protect himself, and so had she.

Heat grew at the base of her throat. Drawing herself up taller, she walked farther into the room.

No more lies.

No more being like her dad.

No more letting fear rule her life.

"Hey," she said softly. She cleared her throat and managed a little more volume. "Hey, everybody, I have something to say."

DeeDee glanced at her. "You do?"

Conversations grew quieter, and several people turned toward Cara.

"My name is Caroline Ann Smith," she said in a loud but unsteady voice. "And I've been hiding my true identity from you."

Carl Cassidy came through the swinging kitchen door, wiping his hands on his white apron. A waitress turned down the radio. And in the back booth, a harried-looking mom handed a fussy toddler a Matchbox car, apparently the perfect appeasement.

Every face in the room was turned toward Cara.

She drew in a deep breath. *Please, God, help me do this.* "I came to Abundance to get away from my past and to start over. I told people I was from Illinois. I dyed my hair red. And I started going by my first name when I'd always used my middle name." She pressed her hands against her sides to stop her fingers from trembling. "But I'm from Kansas, I'm a blonde, and my father is in prison for running a Ponzi scheme."

One by one people shifted in their seats, blinked, or whispered to the person beside them.

"The people he stole from were good, honest people— a lot like you. But I promise you, I had nothing to do with it." She gave her bravest smile. "I hope, I really hope you'll forgive me for keeping all that a secret from you and, now that I'm being my real self, that you'll give me a chance."

No one said a word. The diners glanced at the people they sat with, at the people at the counter, at people across the room.

Cara's heart raced. Her determination and momentary courage drained. The shaking in her hands intensified. She clasped them behind her back and squeezed them tightly together, then looked from one person to the next.

Please. Someone. Anyone. Accept me.

Silence.

Her breath came heavy, and she clenched her fists, digging her nails into her palms. Any time now the nasty comments would start—the name calling, the suggestion that she had money hidden in a Swiss bank account, the classic "like father, like daughter."

Then Carl Cassidy angled his head to one side. He studied her, gave her a thumbs up, and began to clap. The harried-looking mom joined him. And, a fraction of a second later as if on cue, the rest of the diners did too. A long-haired guy in the back even flashed her the peace sign.

A wash of adrenaline flowed through Cara. She raised one hand to her mouth and clutched DeeDee's arm with the other.

DeeDee grabbed Cara's hand and squeezed.

Tears filled Cara's eyes. Her shoulders sagged as she leaned on DeeDee.

Her secret was out. Everyone knew.

And it didn't matter.

In spite of her dad, in spite of her lies, she had been forgiven. Accepted. Allowed a fresh start.

Then, bit by bit, people stopped clapping, and conversations resumed. Carl stepped back into the kitchen. The harried mom and the hippie and all the other diners returned to their meals.

DeeDee led Cara to the counter. "We need three cinnamon rolls to go," she said to Janelle.

Janelle gave Cara a gentle smile and disappeared into

the kitchen.

Still stunned, Cara sank onto a stool and stared at the sign behind the counter. "Today's Homemade Pies: Chocolate Cream, Blackberry, Key Lime."

Snippets of conversation rose above the low hum, like bits of flotsam raised by ocean waves.

"After what Deborah Hamlin told me about how sweet she is, I can't believe they would suspect her."

"She'd only been in town a couple weeks. What were the police thinking?"

"I heard all about her father. I feel sorry for her. My own dad was no prize."

"I was talking with Patsy and T.J. at the post office. I agree with Patsy. What happened to that poor girl is horrible. It's no way to welcome a newcomer to Abundance."

With every comment, Cara's chest grew lighter.

Will, his father, and DeeDee had found the evidence to free her. The whole Hamlin family had helped convince the town to accept her. And God had given her the courage to tell the truth and be the real, authentic Caroline Ann Smith.

She hadn't had that type of courage back in Spottsville. She'd felt hurt and ashamed of her father and guilty for her unwitting role in his crimes. And so...so very worthless.

Will was right, she was sure, when he said that some people back in Spottsville needed an outlet for their anger at her father and had focused that anger on her. But had she brought on part of her suffering herself? Had some people in Spottsville treated her cruelly because she acted guilty? Had she become her own biggest enemy by giving her fear so much power that it almost became an entity working against her?

If she'd just told the whole truth from the first day she'd arrived in Abundance, people might have accepted her. She'd never know for sure.

She did know, however, that she wasn't lying anymore.

She'd been so afraid of people learning about her past, so sure no one would like her if they knew. But what she'd really wanted all along, even though she hadn't realized it, was for people to know what her father had done and like her anyway.

And, now that she'd had the courage to be honest, they did.

A thud rang out, followed by a cry of pain.

"Stupid copier," someone muttered.

On the back stairs of city hall, almost to the second floor, DeeDee froze. "Was that Imogene?"

Cara tightened her grip on the container of cinnamon rolls. Then she and DeeDee hurried up the last three steps and down the hall to the copy room.

Imogene leaned against the copier, one shoe off, rubbing her foot. She looked up. "I'm so glad you're here. I've just learned news about Francine, and I'm dying to tell you."

DeeDee pointed at Imogene's foot. "Are you hurt?"

Imogene brushed aside the question and slid her shoe back on. "Cara, never think for a minute we don't need you here. Kicking that copier didn't help one bit." She pointed to a printed sheet stuck halfway out.

"It probably only needs time to cool down." Cara eased out the offending page, hot as a cup of freshly poured coffee, and turned off the machine. "What's the news?"

"Apparently Francine stole the money for her son, Dominic. Dom's had a drug problem for years, but I never realized it was that serious. Little by little, Francine and her husband have given him their life savings. After they told him no more money was available, he went to Kansas City and borrowed from a loan shark. Francine thought she had to come up with the money or they'd hurt him. She said she planned to put it all back as soon as she could."

"Poor Francine. What a position to be in," DeeDee said.

Imogene shook her head. "That boy has had problems ever since he caused that wreck back in high school that killed Gary Edwards."

Cara's heart skipped a beat. She leaned closer. Had she heard right? "Gary Edwards?"

"He was a good kid," Imogene said. "And it was such a shame when he died. Dom was drunk and should never have been driving. Gary ran off the road trying to avoid a collision with him. Crashed into a tree and died. Dom stopped, saw that Gary was dead, and left before the police ever got there. And both families covered it up because they thought Dom felt bad enough already. I've always believed the guilt drove him to start taking drugs."

"Are you sure? Dom caused the wreck?" Cara said.

"I'm sure." Imogene fingered her gold necklace. "Francine told DeeDee and me years ago." She twisted the gold chain, then released it. "I shouldn't have said anything to you. I wasn't thinking."

"No, no, you should have. I needed to hear this. And, if it's okay with you, there's someone I need to tell, someone who has lived with guilt for years, believing that wreck was their fault," Cara said.

"Oh, my," Imogene said. "Yes, go tell them the truth. I'm pretty sure it's all going to come out now anyway. We can eat the cinnamon rolls when you get back."

"Thank you," Cara said, and she dashed toward the stairs.

Chapter Seventeen

"Will!" Cara ran into his office.

"Um, hi, Cara," Will said, his fingers still on the keys of his typewriter. It was great to see her, but what was she doing here now? "We send the Friday edition to press in—"

"I'll talk fast, but this is important." She shut the door and turned back toward him, her now-blond hair swirling out.

It better be fast. He was crazy about this woman, but he was on deadline. He didn't have time to chat.

"You weren't responsible for Gary's wreck," she said.

This again? "I know you think I was only a kid, but—"

"Dom Young was drunk and ran him off the road."

"That's not possible." He turned to face her directly. "I would have known. Everyone would have known. He would have been arrested."

"The police never knew. The two families covered it up to spare Dom any more suffering."

A sick sensation hit Will's stomach. Could it be true? Could Dom really have caused the wreck? "Are you sure?"

"I'm sure. Imogene said Francine told her and DeeDee years ago."

Will slumped back against his chair and ran a hand over his mouth. Dom was responsible for Gary's death. Not him. Not him.

Like a distant scene becoming more visible as the morning fog cleared, the idea grew more tangible in his mind. Dom had drunk a lot in high school. And he and Will hadn't been great friends, but Dom had seemed different their senior year.

And the fact that Gary's parents wouldn't talk about the wreck made sense. They probably didn't want anyone talking about it. They wanted the truth kept quiet.

They had no way of knowing he'd felt Gary's death was his fault.

All these years he'd felt guilty. Miserable, sometimes. For no reason. Because of a lie.

All these years.

And all these years he'd seen himself as the trained investigator, the inquiring journalist, but missed the real story the whole time.

It took Cara moving to town to find the truth and bring him peace.

"Are you okay?" Cara said.

"Yeah, just shocked." He came out from behind the desk and took her hands in his. "You...you...thank you."

Her eyelashes fluttered down, and she gave a half shrug. "You're welcome." She looked back up at him, and her voice trembled with emotion. "I couldn't let you go on feeling guilty for something that wasn't your fault. Not for a minute longer."

Like water releasing from a dam, the realization of how much she cared flowed through him. What had he ever done to deserve such a woman?

He'd thought he was in love with his last girlfriend. Thought their relationship ended because she didn't want to live in Abundance. But perhaps it ended because he never felt close enough to tell her about Gary. Because deep down he never believed she'd understand.

But Cara was different.

She understood.

And the feelings he had for her were different too. Stronger. Deeper. The kind of feelings that lasted a lifetime.

The back of his throat grew thick, and he pulled her toward him and kissed her.

In a heartbeat, she closed the distance between them, fitting perfectly into his arms.

His senses filled with the softness of her lips, the silkiness of her dress, the warmth of her skin. The happiness of simply being near her. For a half-second, the thought that he needed to proofread the front-page weather forecast wisped through his mind, but then it melted away.

He buried his hands in her hair and scattered kisses down her jawline until he deviated from his path and claimed her lips again. Her lips. Her sweet, sweet lips. He could kiss them for—

Someone knocked on the door.

Cara backed away and ran a hand over her dress, smoothing it. Her cheeks were pink, and her eyes shone.

She was enough to make a man forget all about the Friday edition. So gorgeous. So amazing…

Another knock came at the door.

Will gave his head a quick shake as if the action might re-engage his brain. "I guess I'd better get back to work."

"Me too." She took a step toward him, brushed her lips once more over his, and then slipped out the door.

He stared at the place where she'd been, where now Velma stood holding a pasted-up editorial page.

"Your editorial is three lines too long." Velma thrust the page toward him. "And wipe that lipstick off your face. We're on deadline." She gave a birdlike jerk of her head, spun on her heel, and strode toward the composing room.

Will scrubbed the back of his hand over his lips.

Time to put out the paper.

It had only been four days.

Four days since Friday, when Cara told Will the truth about what had happened to Gary. It seemed like longer, perhaps because he felt so different.

He settled into his desk chair and picked up an editorial he'd been working on.

He was doing the same tasks, but he was no longer using the newspaper to ease his guilt. No longer trying to make up for the lie he'd thought contributed to Gary's death. Sure, he still wanted the *News* to be a good paper, a pillar of democracy, but he didn't feel the same personal pressure. The goal of honest reporting had changed to be more aspiration than atonement, a shift that oddly made him more excited about his work, more hopeful that he could keep Dad from selling the paper.

He read through the editorial, marking a few revisions. His office door was open, and the smell of Russell's burger and fries, fresh from Cassidy's, floated in. Kirk talked a bit too loudly on the phone, taking down golf scores. Someone—possibly Velma judging from the even rhythm—was typing quickly, as if trying to get down a great idea. Nothing unusual, just another day at the paper. But a good day.

Things still weren't perfect. At least once a day, when Will walked through the newsroom, Velma caught his eye and pointedly glared across her pristine desk at Kirk's fortress of piled paper. But it was just playground squabbling. They might each have their quirks, but underneath, they shared the same values. All in all, the newsroom felt right, the way it was supposed to. Like a team serving the community.

Then a phone rang out in the newsroom, and Kim answered.

"I'm sorry," she said. "We don't have any extra copies of the Sunday edition. It sold out."

That issue had included an in-depth article by Russell and Velma, detailing how Francine had embezzled more than ten thousand dollars from the city. Velma had even gotten a quote from Francine, explaining that she'd taken the money to help her son. Everyone in town had wanted the full details. And the *News* had them, along with a story Will had found on the wire about the effects of illegal drug use on family members, a story he had hoped would help people see Francine and her husband with compassion. And it had. Already someone had started a collection to pay for Francine's legal expenses. Will was mentioning it in his editorial.

Any minute now, Dad was coming in. Will couldn't wait to tell him about the sell-out edition. Hopefully, it would help with the conversation they needed to have.

Because despite all that was going well, the *News* faced a big problem. Staffing. Cyndi, of course, was gone. Encouraged by her parents, she was spending the rest of the summer filling in for a camp counselor who'd developed mono.

And soon Russell would be gone too.

Dad had approved replacing Russell but balked at the other position. "You said yourself that Cyndi wasn't any help," he'd said. "And you've been fine all summer."

Somehow, Will had to get Dad to see that the *News* needed to return to the staffing level it had when Hal was the editor.

"Will." Dad knocked on the door.

"Hey, Dad. C'mon in."

Dad took the chair across the desk. "I heard about the sell-out edition." His eyes were filled with pride.

"We never would have figured out that story without your help."

"You would have done just fine," Dad said. "But I can see why you enjoy this business."

"Do you want to be more involved, maybe write a weekly column?"

"Nah, I've got to take care of the herd. At least I'd been careful about isolating that replacement heifer, and it was the only animal we lost to brucellosis. But I've got a fence that needs mending over in the southeast corner of the farm. But back to the paper"—he gestured upstairs and his eyes sparkled—"I met with Veronica."

"And…?"

"And The Food Barn is closing for a reason. Herbst Grocery chain is opening a store here. Veronica's already been talking with them. She says they'll be doing a sizable Sunday insert and a two-page spread every Wednesday, a much bigger ad buy than The Food Barn ever made."

Will let out a delighted laugh. "That's excellent!"

"And she's gotten two other new ads that she says are directly attributable to those extra features you've had on the front page. She says people love those." Dad sat up taller as if he'd written one himself. "That article Kirk wrote about the new gym prompted the owners to take out a weekly ad."

"That's great, Dad." Will shifted in his chair. "But you know that's not why Kirk wrote that article, right?"

"I know. The other new advertiser was drawn in by your article on Alice Butler. No financial connection at all. They said they like the direction the paper is headed and think it will appeal to their shoppers." Dad leaned back. "And I like the direction it's headed too, son."

Will's lungs filled as Dad's words echoed in his brain. The herd was healthy, ad revenues were increasing, and—most importantly—Dad liked what he was doing with the paper. Treasured, treasured words…words he had doubted he'd ever hear. It was the perfect time to talk about staffing. Will scooted forward.

"You better start those interviews to replace Russell," Dad said. "And get an ad running for a full-time replacement for your old reporting position. We need to continue the good news coverage and those front-page features if I'm going to keep the paper."

Will's mouth went dry. "You're not selling it?"

"Nope. With all that advertising from the new grocer, we'll be doing fine. And even if we go through tough times again, we'll find a way to stay afloat. This town needs a locally owned newspaper." Dad gave him a broad grin. "Besides, I've got a topnotch editor-in-chief."

Will's chest expanded, and he felt his cheeks stretch into a huge smile. "Thanks." The newspaper was saved, Dad was pleased with his work, and the editorial department could get back to full staff. Will hadn't even had to ask. "I won't let you down, Dad. I'll get right on the staffing issues."

Dad rose to his feet. "Sounds great. Well, I've got to run to the feed store. Keep up the good work." He gave Will a wave of salute and walked out the door.

Will sat for a long moment, focusing on the sound of Kirk on the phone, the smell of a burger and fries floating in from the newsroom, and the knowledge that great stories were waiting to be edited.

It was not just a good day at the paper. It was an incredible day. The best work day he could have imagined.

And tonight he had a date for dinner at Cara's apartment. He couldn't wait to tell her what Dad had said. And couldn't wait to talk with her about the future.

"Come in!" Cara said as she swung open the door to her apartment. All day she'd been looking forward to having dinner with Will and sharing her news. He was bringing his special spaghetti sauce, and she'd already made a salad after work. Last night, remembering the sad smile he'd given as he returned the empty plate that had held her peanut butter butterscotch crispy treats, she'd whipped up another batch.

He'd clearly stopped at home and changed on the way over. Instead of work clothes, he wore tan shorts and a forest-green Izod that made his hazel eyes look green. His brown hair was rumpled, with one lock flipped the wrong direction.

It was all she could do not to fix it, just for the excuse to touch him. Instead, she led the way—all of four steps— from the hall into her galley kitchen.

Will followed her and, with a flourish, opened a brown paper bag and pulled out a container of store-bought spaghetti sauce and a package wrapped in white butcher's paper. He set them on the counter near her avocado stove. "Ta-da!" he said, giving the package a pat. "Dad's ground beef." He set the empty paper bag on the breakfast bar.

Cara looked at the package, then at the jar of sauce. "Your secret spaghetti sauce recipe has two ingredients?"

"It's the beef that makes it special," he said. "Sorry I didn't have time to cook it before I came over, but it won't take long."

Maybe she wasn't as inept in the kitchen as she'd thought. She'd imagined him chopping garlic and onions and peeling fresh tomatoes. Even she could brown hamburger and open a jar.

She grabbed his hands. "In the meantime, I have news."

"Me too, but"—he angled his head at her as if he could

tell she was too excited to wait—"you first."

"I called my best friends from college, Nora and Bridget, and they're both coming to see me next weekend."

"That's great," Will said. "Why do you sound so surprised?"

She shrugged. "When my dad got arrested, it had been a while since I'd heard from either one of them. We'd lost touch, and I couldn't bring myself to call them." She'd been too ashamed. And so depressed. The fact that they hadn't kept in touch felt like a rejection, like there was no way they would stay her friends if they knew about her dad. "But Bridget hadn't been married that long, and she and her husband had just relocated. She was all wrapped up in him and in her new job. And Nora had just had a baby."

"So they'd both been really busy."

"Exactly." It hadn't been a rejection at all, just life. She pulled a skillet from the cabinet and set it on the counter. "When I called them today, I told them everything. They both felt awful about not being there for me."

"I bet seeing them will be good for you."

"I think you're right. And I can't wait to introduce them to you and show them Abundance." She squeezed his hands. "So what's your news?" She unwrapped the ground beef and tipped it into the pan.

"Dad's not selling the paper. Not now, not ever."

She spun around to face him. "Will, that's huge! How fantastic!"

"I know! I was beginning to worry I'd have to take a job somewhere else." He took the white butcher's paper from her hands, wadded it into a ball, and tossed it in the trash. Then he slid his arms around her waist. "With me secure at the *News*, though, and you happy at city hall— you are happy at city hall, aren't you?" He pulled her closer until she smelled the faint fragrance of his soap, until their bodies were touching.

"I am. People are still adjusting to the news about Francine, but overall, I really like it there."

"Good!" he said, then his tone grew more serious. "Hopefully you and I can both stay in Abundance and spend a lot more time together."

"I'd like that," she said softly.

His gaze intensified.

She stared into his eyes, longing for him to say more.

Silently, he threaded his fingers into her hair, drawing her closer.

She splayed her fingers across his back, almost shivering at the feel of the texture of his shirt and the muscles bunched beneath it.

"Cara Smith," he whispered. He hesitated then pressed a kiss to one side of her neck, just below her ear. "I…"

Her heart pounded.

He kissed below her other ear, his breath caressing her skin. Then he gazed into her eyes. "I love you."

Tingles ran through her, and her chest rose and fell against his. "Oh, Will, I love you too."

He leaned down.

And she raised her lips to his.

Her dream of a new life had come true, a dream made even sweeter by Will's love.

Epilogue

Fifteen months later

What a delicious rehearsal dinner meal.

Will scraped the last bite of mashed potatoes off his plate and popped it in his mouth, savoring the buttery flavor as he looked at the friends and family seated around his parents' dining room and living room. Everyone was dressed up, even his little nephews, even the farmhouse. Cara had gone on and on about how his mom, Deborah, and Patsy had decorated with pumpkins, bittersweet, and red apples.

For him, though, only two things mattered today—having his family here to help him celebrate and the fact that tomorrow Cara would be his bride.

Early last spring, when the redbuds were just peeking out, he'd taken her on a walk to show her his favorite spot on the farm, a slight rise in the land in the northeast corner of the property, a rise with a view of the neighboring farms and the wide, wide blue sky.

She'd stood at the top of a small hill and drawn in a deep breath, as if she could feel the expansive space around them filling her lungs with peace.

He reached down and took her hand. "A beautiful place for a house, don't you think?"

Her eyes narrowed slightly. "It is," she said in a soft voice. "A lovely spot for a home." She stood, not moving a muscle, as if waiting for him to continue.

And he would if only his mouth hadn't gone dry. "Is it—is it a place you might like to live, with me, as my wife?"

"Yes!" She launched herself toward him and wrapped her arms around his neck, and her voice was high and bubbly. "Yes, yes, yes!"

Laughter burst from him. He pulled her closer and kissed her, then spun her around, lifting her feet off the ground, his chest so full it ached.

That spot where they'd stood was now under the back porch of their new home, a home they would share as soon as they returned from their honeymoon in the Ozarks. And tomorrow, this woman, this amazing woman, would be his wife. How had he ever gotten so lucky?

From across the room, Mom waved a hand in the air. "Shall I?" She tipped her head toward the kitchen.

"No, I'll get it," Cara said. She got up and worked her way around people until she disappeared through the doorway.

Mom's eyes shone.

What were those two up to?

A minute later Cara returned, carrying a pumpkin pie and a can of spray whipped topping.

"Aren't we having that fancy apple cheesecake that Deborah read about in a magazine?" Will had actually wanted pumpkin pie all along but decided that a wise man stayed out of most wedding planning.

"Everyone else is. I made this just for us." Cara set the pie on the table. "You get to do the honors." She handed him the can of whipped topping.

"*You* made it? I thought you didn't know how to make desserts except for cookies."

"This was my first pie ever," Cara said. "Your mom helped with the crust."

"Wow. Thanks." Will gave the can of topping a good shake. "I love pumpkin." On top of all the other things that made her incredible, she'd made his favorite pie. He was definitely marrying the right woman. He inhaled the sweet scent of the pie, then sprayed on the topping, spiraling in to cover every inch, and piling it on until it mounded up three inches high.

"Perfect," Cara said with a chuckle. "Exactly the way I like my pie."

He set the can on the table and looked from one person to the next, seeing faces filled with love and welcome for Cara, the newest Hamlin.

All except little Earl Ray.

The boy was sliding out of his seat, his eyes fixed on the can of spray topping, gleaming as if he'd like to see how far it would spray.

One day, Will thought, Mom would let Earl Ray handle the whipped topping.

Today though, it was best to play it safe. Will recapped the can and moved it between him and Cara, out of the boy's reach. He didn't want to be the one to clean whipped cream off the ceiling.

He turned to Cara. "What did I do to deserve pumpkin pie?"

"Well, you did sort of win my heart with all those slices of pie you put on my desk at work, when you thought you were being so sneaky."

Will grinned. She'd seen through him the whole time. He should have known.

"But mostly I remembered your story about you and your brothers," Cara said. "I wanted us to start our marriage with that same attitude. That no matter what, we'd stick together."

Will's throat grew thick, and he looked down at the pie again. "Aw, Cara." It wasn't merely his favorite flavor. It was so much more.

It was someone to count on, someone to share his life, someone to be a team with. He gazed into her eyes, and his heartbeat quickened. "I love you," he said, his voice raw with emotion.

She wrapped one arm around his waist and pulled him close. "I love you too."

The next evening, Cara stood in the vestibule of the Abundance Community Church, out of sight of the congregation, with DeeDee, Imogene, and the twins. She clasped her bouquet with both hands, centering it in front of her.

The bouquet wasn't, as the florist had suggested, a cascade of white like Princess Diana had carried. Sure, Cara had watched the royal wedding in July like everyone else. And her gown did have elements of Diana's, but only the elements Cara loved, like the taffeta fabric and the puffy sleeves.

And Cara's bouquet—red roses, orange dahlias, and a huge, bright yellow sunflower—was hers alone. The dahlias just because they were beautiful. The red roses for their sweet scent and for the true love she had found with Will. And the sunflower because although she'd had a painful experience in Kansas, she'd always loved the tall, happy flowers that symbolized the Sunflower State.

Because she wasn't afraid to show who she was. She wasn't living a lie.

Not anymore.

She was blessed simply being herself.

After attending the Abundance Community Church for more than a year, she understood how rich her life was. She had material blessings like a home, food to eat, and a steady paycheck from her job, working beside DeeDee as an assistant treasurer for Abundance. She had the blessings of Will and his family, the friends she had made, and the fellowship of her new church. Through the Bible study class that Mary taught, Cara had learned that she had the immense blessing of a God who loved her, not just enough to answer her prayers but enough to offer her salvation.

And she had the blessing of the peace she had found after she visited her father in prison. It had taken several letters to convince him, but their time together was important. Now she no longer saw him as the all-powerful, perfect father she had when she was a child or as a manipulative, evil man who'd betrayed her, but as someone who was struggling and deserved forgiveness.

Again and again, she'd seen God bless her life, not always in the time frame she wanted, not always in the manner she wanted, but sometimes in a way that far exceeded anything she could imagine.

Here, where she'd at last had the courage to be herself, she had found what she wanted. She'd been accepted as part of the Hamlin family, as a new member of the Abundance Community Church, and as a citizen of the little town of Abundance, Missouri. A town where she and Will would put down deep roots and hopefully leave a lasting legacy for years to come. She felt valued and loved—by Will and his family and by God.

Suddenly, Imogene peeked out the double doors to the congregation, then bent over, straightened the bows on the back of the twins' burgundy dresses, and smoothed their hair. "Now you girls remember to go slowly," she whispered to them. Then she led them to the double doors and pointed them down the aisle.

DeeDee squeezed Cara's shoulders. "You look beautiful." Her eyes shimmered as if she might cry. "Even prettier than any of the stars on *Dallas*."

"She's absolutely gorgeous." Imogene handed DeeDee a tissue.

"Thank you." Cara squeezed out the words and swallowed back the lump in her throat. "Thank you for everything you've done. For becoming my family here in Abundance." She hugged them both, then ran a hand over the skirt of her gown, took a deep breath, and stepped closer, where she could see through the doorway.

A long white runner, scattered with orange and yellow and red rose petals, stretched before her. Tall white candles shone on each windowsill, accented by miniature pumpkins and red and yellow ribbons. And three candles stood on the altar, trimmed with sunflowers and pumpkins and, here and there, a red rose.

And any minute now...

Yes. The organ music had paused.

Excitement coursed through Cara's veins, and she turned toward Imogene and DeeDee.

The first notes of "The Wedding March" filled the air.

"It's time," DeeDee said. She squeezed Cara's arm and then dashed toward the basement stairs.

The congregation rose to their feet, familiar faces turning toward Cara. Thomas and Mary in the front row, holding Jack and Earl Ray. Nora and Bridget's husbands and Nora's little one. DeeDee's husband. Velma and her husband. Kirk and his family. A little farther back, Rachel with her friends Carl and Janelle Cassidy.

Patsy, who would be singing during the service, sat off to one side near the altar. DeeDee, who would read a scripture passage, slipped in beside her, her cheeks pink from hurrying to the front through the basement of the church.

Near the altar, in simple burgundy satin dresses, stood Cara's bridesmaids, Deborah, Nora, and Bridget.

On the other side were Will's groomsmen, tall and handsome, his brothers T.J. and John and his friend from college, Andy.

Most importantly, there, in the center, was Will. Her

dear, wonderful Will, so handsome in his gray suit. Will, who had rescued her from that horrible jail, who brought her pie and made her laugh, and who loved her in spite of her father's flaws and her own.

His hazel eyes met hers, and her heart filled.

Warmth flowed through her, and she felt as if she were floating down the aisle. The music seemed to grow softer. And everything before her—the bright yellow sunflowers on the altar, the glimmer of the candle flames, even the dear friends and family—all of it fell away. At this moment, none of it mattered, nothing but Will, smiling at her.

With him she'd truly found the love of a lifetime.

A lifetime they'd spend together.

In Abundance.

All of Sally's books are available in paperback and e-book from Amazon. For a complete list, or to sign up for her author newsletter and get a free novella, please visit her website at www.sallybayless.com.

A NOTE FROM THE AUTHOR

Dear Reader,

Thank you for reading *Love of a Lifetime!* I hope you enjoyed Will and Cara's story. I had so much fun revisiting 1980 while I was writing it. Things sure have changed since then, especially with respect to technology. I have to say, although sometimes my printer and I don't get along, I don't miss typewriters one bit!

Luckily, by the time I was an intern reporter at my hometown paper during the summers of 1984 and 1985, we used word processors. As for my days as an intern, I promise I wasn't as bad as Cyndi, but I did get sent over to the police station to write up the police report an awful lot! You'd think that task would be a source of exciting front-page news, but almost always it was a paragraph on page six about a malfunctioning alarm at a local discount store. Even though I didn't break any big stories, I thoroughly enjoyed my time as an intern and learned an awful lot.

While I was writing this story about Cara and her fears, I pondered the role fear has had in my own life—fear of failure, fear of what other people might think, fear of a million things that are out of my control. For me, that last one, not being in control, is often the real issue. I have to remind myself again and again that God is in control, not me. Like Cara, I'm trying to trust Him more and embrace the opportunities He sets before me. If you also struggle with fear, I hope in some small way this story will encourage you.

If you enjoyed this book, I'd be really grateful if you would write a review on Amazon or Goodreads. Those reviews are the best advertising around, and you wouldn't believe how fun it is to get feedback!

I love to hear from readers! If you'd like to say hello, please visit my website at www.sallybayless.com, where you can email me or find me on social media.

Love of a Lifetime is the prequel to the Abundance Series, which is set in the current day. A sample of Book 1 in the series, *Love at Sunset Lake*, is included just a few pages ahead.

Would you like a free copy of another sweet Christian romance set in the little town of Abundance? Sign up for my author newsletter at www.sallybayless.com and get a link to download the holiday novella *Christmas in Abundance* for free in ebook or PDF!

May God bless you,

Sally Bayless

ACKNOWLEDGMENTS

I am incredibly blessed in my writing journey to have help from many, many people. I truly could not do this without them. Any errors that slipped in despite their best efforts are my own.

Thank you to Brian K. Williamson, Chief of the Bullhead City, Arizona, Police Department, who helped me make sure that the police officers in my story acted as they might have in a small town in 1980—perhaps not by the book as it would be done today, but reasonable for the time and place. I am so grateful for his insight and his willingness to help.

Thank you also to Lynnette Bush Clouse of Ohio University's Design and Construction Department, who helped me with architectural details for the Hamlin farmhouse.

Thank you to Dianna Keeney-Jarvis of The Loft Hair & Spa Salon in Athens, Ohio, who helped me decide the most believable hair color for Cara to use when she wanted to change her appearance.

And thank you to Mike Sell, former owner and publisher of the *Monroe City News* in Monroe City, Missouri, who helped me understand the production process of a 1980 small-town newspaper. I had never worked in a newsroom before computers, and his comments were invaluable.

Thank you to my critique partners, Susan Anne Mason and Tammy Doherty. I am so grateful to have you as my "work colleagues" and so blessed to have your advice for making my stories better.

To my beta readers—Betsy Anderson, Carrie Saunders, Jan LeBar, Janice Huwe, Kristina Gerig, Leisa Ostermann, Michelle Blackwell, Stephanie Smith, and my daughter, Laurel Bayless—you all are amazing! You make such wonderful suggestions, you encourage me, and you help my book shine! A special thanks to Laurel, who read this book late in the editing process when I so very much needed another set of eyes to look things over.

Sally Bradley edited this story. It is immensely richer, more readable, and more enjoyable because of her work. As always she pushed me to dig deeper and bring more emotion to my writing. I am so very grateful for her help.

The cover was designed by Jenny Zemanek of Seedlings Design Studio. Truly, having Jenny design my cover is a blessing from God. She is so incredibly talented and such a joy to work with. Thank you, Jenny!

Thank you to my husband, Dave, for all your love and support. And thank you to my son, Michael, who uses his computer skills and artistic eye to help me again and again.

Most importantly, thank you, Jesus, for loving me and giving me stories and the desire to write. May all my words point back to you.

RECIPES

I share this first recipe with a note of warning. When I first made these cookies in 1988, I, um, accidentally ate half of a 9″ x 13″ pan at one sitting. After making several more batches over the next few weeks and eating them far too quickly, I threw the recipe away. About five years ago I found it again online. I've been able to show more restraint than I did in my twenties, but these cookies are still quite addictive.

Peanut Butter Butterscotch Crispy Treats

6 cups crispy rice cereal
1 cup peanut butter
12 oz. butterscotch morsels

Measure the cereal into a bowl to have ready.

In a large pot, melt the peanut butter over medium heat. Add the butterscotch morsels. Stir constantly. Do not overcook or step away from the stove. The morsels burn easily. Remove from heat as soon as the butterscotch morsels are almost melted. Stir a bit more.

Stir in the cereal. Pour into a 9″ x 13″ pan and smooth the top. Refrigerate about an hour. Then cut into squares and eat.

Cassidy's Pie Crust
Makes a top and bottom crust for a 9″ pie

Mix your filling first and have it ready. Then work with the crust as quickly as possible so your hands won't make it warm and sticky.

To make the crust, mix:
2 ½ cups flour
½ cup powdered sugar
1 teaspoon salt

Cut in with pastry cutter until in tiny pieces:
½ cup Crisco
1 stick cold butter

Mix in some ice water a little at a time until the dough forms a ball. Knead lightly and quickly in additional flour until ready to roll out. Grease your pie pan with butter before placing crust in pan.

Janelle Cassidy says that when she makes a crust for a tart pie like her lemon meringue, she increases the powdered sugar to almost ¾ of a cup.

Cassidy's Apple Pie Filling
For a 9" pie

Start with 6-8 tart apples. Jonathan apples are my favorite variety to use, but Granny Smiths will do.

Peel and slice enough apples to fill the pie pan. Do not pile up above the top of the pan.

Sprinkle with:
⅓ cup flour

Stir in:
1 cup sugar
½ cup orange juice
Squirt of lemon juice
Dash of salt
1 scant teaspoon nutmeg
½ teaspoon cinnamon

Prepare the crust and pour the prepared filling into the bottom crust.

Top with:
2 Tablespoons butter, cut into about 8 small pieces.

Add the top crust. Seal the edges, making sure not to pinch them too thin so they won't burn. Cut slits in the top crust. Bake at 425°F for 10 minutes, then at 350°F for 45-60 minutes. When the pie is done, the top crust will be lightly brown.

Pumpkin Pie Filling
For an 8-9" pie

This is not a recipe from 1980. I'm not even sure they had fat free half and half back then. However, this is the pumpkin pie I like best. It is very pumpkin-y, and because the filling is not quite so fattening, I manage to justify eating more mashed potatoes!

Mix in the mixer:
1 15-ounce can pumpkin puree (I like Libby's)
¾ teaspoon ground cinnamon
¼ teaspoon ground cloves
¼ teaspoon ground ginger
⅛ teaspoon ground nutmeg
¾ cup fat-free half-and-half
½ cup sugar
2 eggs, slightly beaten

Prepare your bottom pie crust, then give the pumpkin mixture one more stir. Pour in. Bake at 425°F for 15 minutes, then at 350°F for about 45 minutes. Test for doneness by sticking a sharp knife tip in the filling. If it comes out clean, it is done. After it is cooled, store in the refrigerator. Serve with homemade whipped cream or (as at our house) with spray whipped topping.

ABOUT THE AUTHOR

After many years away, Sally Bayless lives in her hometown in the Missouri Ozarks. She's married and has two grown children. When not working on her next book, she enjoys reading, watching BBC television with her husband, doing Bible studies, swimming, and shopping for cute shoes.

Have you read Book 1 of
The Abundance Series?

If not, please turn the page to read the beginning of

Love at Sunset Lake

Chapter One

Tess Palmer didn't need to be perfect. She only needed to get every detail right.

Every time.

And as a special events caterer, her to-do list this Friday ran for three entire pages of details.

She stopped at a light in a pricey St. Louis suburb and glanced at the clipboard on the console of her van. For the next event, a simple surprise birthday party, she'd gone over her list so many times that the edges of the paper curled. The future of her catering business was at stake, after all.

She drove two blocks farther, passed a row of dogwoods in full bloom at the entrance to a subdivision, and parked as instructed in the client's three-car garage, where her commercial van could be hidden from the guest of honor.

Up since five, Tess had triple-checked the food,

recounted the plates, and examined every tablecloth for spots. She'd even taken more care than normal with her appearance, using a double coating of hairspray to keep her hair in a bun, dousing her white blouse with extra starch, and wearing her newest black pants. This event was going to be a success. She'd make sure of it.

A stack of plates in one arm, she walked to the door that led into the house from the garage and knocked.

Madeleine McCullen pulled the door open wide and, although she was well past sixty-five, fluttered her hands like an excited five year old. "My son just sent a text. His wife doesn't suspect a thing, thinks I'm picking up drive-thru burgers for our lunch." She ushered Tess into a huge kitchen.

"We can definitely do better than drive-thru." Tess set the plates on the island and flashed an encouraging pre-event smile.

A silver-haired Peter Pan, at five-foot-nothing and maybe a hundred pounds, Madeleine made Tess—five seven and more on the sturdy side—feel like a Clydesdale.

But Clydesdales know how to work, and Tess was all about work.

Madeleine tapped Tess's stack of plates with the click of a long, manicured nail. "You've got more of those?"

"Three more loads. Plenty for fifty guests."

Madeleine stepped closer, surrounded by a cloud of magnolia perfume. The hot-pink sequins on her blouse caught the light. "Dear..." Her voice hit the same too-sweet note that it held each time she'd called to change the menu.

Tess gripped the edge of the granite countertop,

stomach tightening. A week ago, she'd made it clear that everything had to be final, including the number of guests. "Fifty people, right?"

"Well…" Guilt flashed across Madeleine's eyes. "My other daughter decided to fly in from Dallas. With her husband and teenage son."

Tess released her death hold on the granite. "Three more people? No problem. I always allow ten-percent extra." Paying attention to detail, planning for overages like this, riding herd on indecisive clients like Madeleine—it had taken four years, but Tess was getting good at catering.

"I told her she could bring her in-laws," Madeleine said. "And her best friend."

Tess stopped congratulating herself.

"And their families." Madeleine slipped the words in soft and low, as if that made the news easier to take.

It didn't.

The nerves in Tess's stomach contracted into a knot. "How many people total?" She tried to sound calm but failed.

"I added it up." Madeleine pulled a small piece of paper from her pocket. "Sixty-five. That's why I think you'll need more plates."

With effort, Tess kept her mouth shut. Sixty five? Fifteen extra people? Plates were the least of her problems.

She needed an additional dessert, more appetizers, and more drinks, all ready to serve in less than four hours. And her kitchen was thirty minutes away.

But she had to pull this off. In catering, there were no second chances, and she was counting on referrals from

Madeleine to boost her business over the hump, safely into the world where she'd make a solid profit every year.

"Excuse me. I need to make a call." Tess backed toward the garage. "And make sure I have more, um, plates."

"I thought so." Now smiling, Madeleine smoothed her gray pixie cut. "Good thing I asked about them when you first got here."

Tess gave a tight nod.

"Hey, where's my beautiful bride of forty-seven years?" A barrel-chested older man wearing a green golf shirt with a country club logo walked in from the garage and blocked Tess's escape.

Madeleine's brown eyes sparkled. "Right here, Harry."

He wrapped her in a huge hug and then, one arm still around her sequined shoulders, beamed at her as though she was his own personal Miss America.

Tess looked away and braced herself for the all-too-familiar wave of sadness. Now was not the time to dwell on what was missing in her life. She had a food crisis to handle. "I'll be back." In the garage, she climbed into the van and wiped the moisture from her palms on her pants. Then she pulled out her cell phone, dialed Rose, and hurriedly explained about Madeleine's extra guests.

"How are we supposed to feed heavy hors d'oeuvres and birthday cake to another fifteen people?" Rose's voice shot up an octave on the last word.

"I don't know. But remember what the sous-chef at her country club said?"

"'If we get Madeleine's approval, the jobs will roll in,' but—"

"No 'buts.' We have to do this." Sometimes when a job went off course, Tess had to push Rose past panic. "It's a buffet. That helps."

"True," Rose said with less tension, more resignation.

"I'll take stuff inside and then pick up more crackers and some fancy olives. Call you from the store."

The second Tess hung up, her phone rang.

An unfamiliar number with the area code for Sunset Lake, out in north-central Missouri, where Great-Aunt Leticia had lived.

The reality of her death two days ago swept over Tess anew.

But the call wasn't from the funeral home or the minister. She knew those numbers.

With exactly three hours and twenty-seven minutes until the McCullen party, anybody else would have to wait.

She let the call roll to voice mail and unloaded the rest of the food, squeezing what she had to into Madeleine's refrigerator, then backed out of the driveway and headed toward the highway. Ten minutes later she reached her exit and steered up the off-ramp.

On the incline, the van slowed dramatically, even when she punched her foot on the gas. *What was going on?*

The van inched up the ramp, finally reaching the top. Back on level ground, it drove normally again.

Tess blew out an exasperated breath. Once this event was finished, she'd have to get the engine checked. Silver Platter Catering couldn't survive without wheels, even if van repair wasn't in the budget. But how was she going to pay for it? Forget about borrowing from family. Her brother, the boy genius, was doing his residency in pediatrics and struggling with student loans. And asking Mom for money would only lead to a resounding no, followed by a discussion of Tess's failures.

Tess snagged a parking spot, grabbed her phone, and called Rose. "I played with a new ice cream last night, Coconut Lemon Bliss. We can have a server put mini scoops in glass dessert cups at the end of the buffet.

"I saw that in the freezer."

Wait, she hadn't made that much ice cream. "Why don't you crush some graham crackers to line the bottom of the cups?"

"Okay. And I found dough for those yummy cheese straws."

"Perfect. Start those. I'll be there soon."

An hour and a half later, with small culinary miracles complete, Tess turned off the highway and headed back to the McCullens'.

Rose sat in the passenger seat, cheeks still pink from their frantic loading. Although a year younger than Tess, Rose appeared older than her twenty-six years, the toll of late nights as the single mother of a toddler. She balanced the birthday cake on her lap, and the scent of its buttercream frosting filled the front of the van.

The rest of the food—enough for sixty-five—was secured in the back.

"I can't believe we did it." Rose pushed her dark bangs off her forehead. "I'm glad you had that new ice cream made. It's amazing, like nothing I ever tasted."

"Thanks." Tess looked over at Rose. "But Madeleine's daughter-in-law isn't the only one with a birthday today, and don't think I've forgotten. I didn't have time to give it to you, but I got you a present. It's nothing huge, just a season pass to the zoo for you and Charlie. I figure he's old enough—"

"Nothing huge?" Rose's voice grew higher and filled with emotion. "It's way more than you should have done."

"Nonsense. You know I love birthdays. And you're one of my best friends." A bit of an understatement. Tess's old friends had moved to another galaxy, orbiting husbands and babies. If she didn't count clients and wait staff, on most days, Rose was the only person Tess talked to.

Not that Rose knew that. When she wasn't at Silver Platter, Rose spent time with her son and her mommy friends.

When Tess wasn't at Silver Platter, she made checklists.

"I'm so glad we work togeth—" Tess glanced down at the floorboard, then at the huge hill they were climbing— or trying to climb. Only a fourth of the way up. She jammed her foot down.

Instead of an encouraging *vroom*, the engine made a weak moan.

Useless. Her pulse sped and she shot a look at Rose.

"Are we out of gas?" Lines formed around the edges of Rose's mouth.

Tess pointed at the full gas gauge. "And I was fine on the highway where it was flat."

"We're at least two miles away." Rose's tone said she'd given up, like it might as well be two hundred miles.

Tess yanked the steering wheel hard to the right and

turned onto a side street. Not. Giving. Up. "We'll cut through by The Ice Cream Station and avoid that big hill. Maybe we can make it that way."

"Leave it to you to know a back way past a place that sells ice cream."

In spite of her worry, Tess grinned. She did sample a lot of ice cream. But she liked to think of it as research.

On the side street, the van eased along, almost as if nothing was wrong. Two minutes later they reached a stop sign. Beyond it, the road dipped, then climbed again.

Rose leaned forward, peering ahead.

Tess tightened her grip on the steering wheel. They only had that hill and about half a mile to go. But with the time they'd lost cooking for fifteen more guests, there was no way to carry all the food in on foot. She studied the road ahead and looked back at Rose. "If I get up enough speed going down this hill, maybe I can coast up the next one."

Rose lowered her head and began to pray under her breath.

Tess kept her focus on the road, not heaven. God probably wouldn't help her, but maybe he would intervene—for Rose.

Jaw tight, Tess floored the gas.

The old van raced down the hill, bottomed out, and began to climb. Three-fourths of the way up, however, gravity took hold.

"C'mon, c'mon." Tess's heart pounded. She sucked in a breath and pressed harder on the gas, straining her thigh muscle to ram her black clog against the floorboard.

Yard by sluggish yard, the van crept up the hill.

With a jolt, as if fueled by its dying breath, it rose the

final inches to the crest.

Tess exhaled. "We made it."

Rose slumped against the seat. "Once we unload, I'll call my cousin's friend and see if he can look at the van tomorrow."

"Thanks."

Tess turned into the McCullen driveway and, with one hand, lifted the collar of her blouse off her chest to let in some cool air. Time to act like nothing had happened. Time to wow Madeleine McCullen and ensure the future of Silver Platter Catering.

Six hours later, packing up in the kitchen as the last guest left, Tess leaned against the counter and caught her breath. In spite of fifteen extra guests, her ancient van, and the hills, the party had been a success.

Madeleine walked in, looking less fresh-from-the-salon, more droopy pixie.

Though Tess and her staff did the heavy lifting, being a good hostess was exhausting.

"You were fantastic." Madeleine's eyes met Tess's, her sincerity clear. "Those crab things. And that ice cream... Give me a week or two to talk you up, and your phone will be ringing off the hook."

Excitement filled Tess's chest like a swig of carbonated soda. Exactly what she needed—good reviews that would bring in more catering jobs. Her hard work would pay off in success. "Thank you, Madeleine. Your recommendation will mean a lot."

"You've got it." Madeleine rubbed her lower back. "I'm going upstairs to take something for this. Just show yourself out when you're done." She slid off her pink mules, picked them up, and padded toward the hall, leaving behind a faint scent of magnolias.

Tess bundled up the tablecloths, the last load. Now she only needed to help Rose strap the trays in the van.

Oh, the call she hadn't taken. Probably some question about the funeral. With Dad long dead and Leticia's brother in the hospital, Tess had ended up in charge.

She pulled up her voice mail and hit Play.

"Hello, this is Jewel, from the law firm of Redmond and Sons. Mr. Al Redmond would like you to come by Monday right after the funeral for Leticia Palmer. You're named as a beneficiary in her estate."

All of Sally's books are available in paperback and e-book from Amazon. For a complete list, or to sign up for her author newsletter and get a free novella, please visit her website at www.sallybayless.com.

Made in the USA
Las Vegas, NV
22 November 2021

35063545R00115